Those Eyes

Those Eyes

Rom Wills
Wills Publishing

Those Eyes

© Copyright 2014, 2015

By

Romuald P. Wills

Romuald P. Wills

romwills@aol.com

ISBN – 13 978-0692387795

ISBN – 10 069238779X

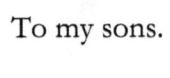

Chapter 1

Rhythmic motion...
Back and forth...
Around in a circle...
Dark and light...
Light and dark...
Grinding...
Grinding...
A symphony of movement and energy building from a single flute to a triumphant overture electrifying the senses. The

explosions of multiple orgasms were intense as energy traveled up the spine of the young Japanese woman as she became immersed in a sea of ecstasy. Basking in the afterglow she looked over at her partner's chocolate skin. His well-muscled body, strong jaw line, high cheekbones, and almond eyes framed by curly eyelashes were always enough to keep her aroused.

"You're barely breathing hard," the woman said between breaths. "I feel like I've run a marathon."

The man ran a finger along his partner's waist. "Have you?"

"With you…always. How do you…do it?"

"I eat well Yumi-chan."

"Don't play with my heart Danny. You talk like we can be more than bed buddies."

"Who knows," Danny grinned.

"You know I'm going back to Japan. Using "chan" with my name implies closeness."

Danny flashed perfectly white teeth. "We do get pretty close."

"Oh…you know what I mean," Yumi smiled. "There's something about you…I don't know…especially your eyes. They're so compelling. Who are you?"

"I'm magic." Danny gently stroked Yumi's eyebrows. "Do you want me to show you a trick?"

Yumi responded softly. "Yes."

"Come here." Danny pulled Yumi to him and kissed her deeply, reigniting the fire in her.

****

"So here you are Yumi." Danny and Yumi were standing at the entrance of her apartment building.

Yumi smiled at Danny. "It was great. You were great."

"Good luck on your paper."

"Thank you. When will I see you again?"

"Give me a call Yumi." Danny gave Yumi a peck on her lips.

"See you later magic-man." Yumi watched Danny walk back to his Blue Ford Mustang. He was wearing a lightweight black sweater that clung like a second skin to his six foot muscular frame along with light grey slacks. "Definitely see you later."

****

The crowd at *Riley's Place* was loud and drunk as always. Despite the crowd, Danny was able to find a small table in the corner. As he usually did on his visits to the club he ordered a pitcher of beer and some popcorn. Danny took in everything around him. The men were of all classes and incomes. Some were trying to look like playas with their cigars and wads of cash in their hands. Some looked like thugs hardened by the school of hard knocks. The rest looked like they were happy to be this close to naked women.

The dancers came out one at a time in provocative attire. Some were slim, some were voluptuous, some were tall, and some were short. Some were bottom heavy, some were top heavy. All had screamingly erotic auras. They took off their clothes and danced to the beats of the pulsating music. Danny simply watched and occasionally nodded his head as if he was in a state of trance. For 45 minutes he was in a state of relaxation until the DJ announced, "Now coming to the stage…show some love for Steam!"

At that moment the men in the club went crazy. As the music pumped a woman came out in four-inch heels, a dress that stopped halfway on her butt and a fireman's hat. Steam had light-brown skin, relatively small breasts, and the legs of a Broadway dancer. The crowd began to yell as Steam began her slow erotic dance. Men rushed the stage to tip her before she finished undressing. Steam's shoulder length hair slightly framed her slim face with its slightly upturned nose and heart-shaped lips. Her most beautiful feature was her eyes. Though an ordinary shade of brown there was something about her eyes which captivated men and women alike. They seemed to be both wise and distant at the same time.

When she finished disrobing the energy level in the room went higher as the crowd got a full look at Steam's perfectly round butt and hips. Men were so transfixed on Steam's lower body that her relatively small breasts were virtually ignored. It made her more endearing. As Steam danced her movements were like a magnet, which drew streams of energy from the men in the club. Steam moved as if she was oblivious to the attention. She was in her own reality. Then as she moved around on the stage her eyes caught sight of Danny. For a few seconds Steam's eyes locked onto Danny's eyes. In a brief moment nothing was said but everything was understood. The expression of neither Danny nor Steam changed and yet within them a great deal was happening.

Danny felt like a deer frozen in the headlights of a car without brakes. A stream of energy so powerful hit that he was taken by surprise.

Outwardly no reaction.

Inwardly a volcano erupted.

Slowly Danny reached into his back pocket to get his wallet and pulled out a twenty-dollar bill. Danny was moved, no, he thought. He was commanded to give Steam money.

The immovable object had been moved.

As he walked to the stage, Danny felt pulled as if by a powerful magnet. When he reached the stage Steam paused to allow Danny to tip her.

"Thank you," Steam smiled slightly.

"Come to my table," Danny said softly with his mouth. *You will come to my table*, he commanded with his eyes.

"When I'm through." Steam looked into Danny's eyes and continued to dance.

****

"I can't believe he tipped you. He never tips," Destiny said as she put on shorts and a vest on her slim body.

"And he gave you a twenty. He musta been saving for you." Thunder rested her voluptuous body on a chair.

Steam was putting on a tight form fitting spandex mini dress. "He never tips?"

"Oh that's right. You haven't seen mister cheapskate pretty

11

boy. Chile let me tell you. One set I did everything but sit on that dude's face and he just looked at me with those pretty eyes of his like I was disturbing his groove." Destiny laughed as she adjusted her costume.

"You musta enchanted him 'cause I ain't never seen a man get off his ass like that. You worked a mojo on him. You into that voodoo shit?" Thunder asked.

"I did something," Steam said quietly. "He wants me to come to his table."

Thunder laughed. "Well get on with ya bad self. Break off a little sumptin, sumptin."

"Girl you crazy," Steam said as she went out to the floor.

Steam moved through the crowd as if in a dream. She said something to all the men who tipped her and even to the ones who didn't. Despite the requests of several men Steam never lost sight of her objective, Danny. She was like a moth drawn to a flame burning amidst a dark abyss.

Steam reached Danny's table. "Hello."

"What's up? Have a seat. Would you like something to drink?" Danny stood up and offered Steam a seat.

Steam sat down and crossed her legs. "I don't drink. Thank you though,"

"You're really something," Danny said as he sat down.

"Thank you. I must be since the girls tell me you never tip."

"I got a rep huh?"

"That's putting it mildly. You don't like the other girls?"

12

"They're all right. It just takes a lot to move me. I figure I'm doing my part by paying admission and buying beer."

"So what's different about me?"

"One it's your legs. Even now it's taking all my willpower to keep from looking down."

"You must have a strong will because you haven't taken your eyes off of my face."

"You have a beautiful face."

"You're different. You not like the other men in here. I can't put my finger on it." Steam liked how Danny's Caesar haircut framed his handsome face.

"I'm just a hardworking man looking to unwind. I'm recharging my batteries so to speak. You ladies generate a lot of heat."

"Thank you. Maybe you should tip more and you'll really get charged up."

Danny grinned. "When you put it like that…"

Steam barely suppressed a gasp when she looked at Danny's eyes and smile.

"The fellas look like they are jealous you're spending time with me. Maybe they should give you twenties too," Danny said.

"Please, they'll give me credit cards if I allow them to," Steam said matter of factly. "Are you hanging around for my next set?"

"I wish I could but I have something to do in the morning."

"Will you come back?"

"I'll be back."

"See you later…that's funny. I don't know your name."

"Danny Code."

"Wow, you sound like an action hero. Is your life exciting?"

"Depends on who you ask."

Steam stood up. "Hmmmm. I have to get backstage. Hope to see you again soon."

"You will."

Steam left the table lost in her thoughts until a voice interrupted her.

"Hey boo how come you didn't stop and talk with us?" A big fat man with a Ravens jersey and jeans asked out loud.

"Tip me more and I will," Steam said with slight grin as she headed for the dressing room.

"Han, don't even worry 'bout that freak," a slim man with a scraggly goatee said.

Han was pissed. "She can't be walking past me like that."

"Let it go dawg."

"Here that bamma come she was hollering at," Han said as Danny walked by and looked briefly at Han and kept walking.

"Whassup with that nigga? He don't know." Han was very agitated.

"Better leave him alone dawg. You see that bamma's eyes? They look like they done seen some shit. Don't even stress over it. Let's keep checking out these broads."

****

Steam woke up slowly in her small efficiency in Northeast, DC. She was still tired after putting in a hard night's work at the club the night before. She made 367 dollars in tips, which for her was a slow night. No matter, she thought, meeting Danny made the night worthwhile. Now it was time to see her main man.

Steam rolled out of bed and immediately walked to the bathroom and turned on the shower. She always took long showers the morning after dancing. The water washed away the energy of the hundreds of men who lusted after her. After 30 minutes Steam got out of the shower feeling invigorated. Water always did that for her. After drying off, Steam sat cross-legged on the middle of her rug and began to breathe rhythmically as she did her meditation practice. After another 30 minutes Steam got off the floor and put her clothes on as she occasionally glimpsed at the picture of her man on her coffee table. She put on a loose pair of jeans, a large T-shirt, and a pair of white sneakers. Steam then got a lightweight jacket and a pair of glasses to cover her beautiful face, and pulled her into a ponytail. She was ready to see her man.

****

"Good afternoon honey. How are you today?" the mature woman asked as she opened the door for Steam.

"I'm fine Ms. Foster, ma'am. Where's my man?"

"I call him. Solomon!!!"

In response a short plump teenaged boy came down the steps with eyes gleaming and a broad smile.

"Lish!" Solomon yelled at Steam as he ran and hugged her.

"Alicia, he always lights up when he sees you," Ms. Foster said while radiating maternal energy.

Alicia kissed Solomon. "How's my teddy bear brother been

15

behaving?"

"F-F-fine. I've been good," Solomon answered.

"My, you are fine today." Alicia looked at her brother's clothes. He was wearing an Eagles jersey, jeans, and a new pair of Jordan's she bought him. "You always did out dress me, Solly."

"Okay," Solomon said.

"You're supposed to say, 'thank you' when people compliment you," Alicia said in a motherly fashion.

"Okay."

"Boy!" Alicia said sternly and then broke out into a smile. She could never be mad at her 'man.' "Ms. Foster, how has Solly been doing in school."

Ms. Foster beamed with pride. "He's doing great. The teachers really rave about his art. They say he may be a savant."

"W-What's a s-s-savant, Lish?" Solomon asked.

Alicia smiled at her brother. "It means you're real smart."

"I'm not smart, Lish. Not like you." Solly looked sad.

"Don't let me hear you say that again Solomon." Alicia lifted Solomon's head. "We're both smart in different ways."

Solomon smiled. "Okay,"

"Where are y'all going today," Ms. Foster asked.

"We're going to the movies and walk around the mall," Alicia answered.

"W-walk around the mall," Solomon repeated.

Chapter 2

"How's my two favorite customers doing?" Elias Robbins asked as Alicia and Solomon walked into his store, *Robbins Books*. He walked around the checkout counter with his slim 6' 2" frame to hug both Alicia and Solomon. He was dressed casually in a T-shirt and jeans.

"You call all your customers your favorite," Alicia said while breaking the embrace with Elias.

"All y'all my favorite as long as you're spending some duckets."

Alicia smiled. "All about the money baby."

"I know you're not going there." Elias gave Alicia a high five. "What movie y'all going to see?"

"W-W-Were gonna see *The Playa*," Solomon answered.

"Maybe I need to go see that one bruh. I could learn something," Elias smirked.

Alicia rubbed her friend's arm. "Don't start that baby. You know you fine." She did think Elias was very fine with his oval face and aquiline nose. With his curly hair he looked East African. She really liked his eyes which were a shade lighter than his coffee colored skin.

"Your sisters don't agree with you but as long as they spend money in here it's all good."

"You so silly. Any good books come in?" Alicia scanned the interior of the store.

"There's a book on Kemetic spiritual practices coming in next week. I'll reserve a copy for you if you like."

"Do that for me baby. I still need to finish that last book you sold me. That brotha was deep."

"Didn't I tell you? That bamma broke some things down. I thought I knew some stuff before but dang! My man took it to a whole nutha level."

"The movie's about to start. I'm out baby. We'll stop by afterwards. Peace." Alicia gave Elias a warm hug and left with her brother.

As Alicia and Solomon walked out the entrance, a woman walked past them into the store. She was tall and quite voluptuous.

She was wearing a dark blue business jacket and skirt with stockings and pumps. Her hair was swept back into a bob. Everything about the woman suggested class as even her makeup complemented her brown skin. She walked directly to Elias.

"Good Afternoon, Mr. Robbins. I hope this is not a bad time," the woman said in a clear and precise voice which pronounced each word clearly like a TV news anchorperson.

"Not at all," Elias said to the woman whose slight smile showed adorable dimples set against a round face. He looked at his two young female workers. "Hold it down out here. I have some business matters to discuss with Ms. Jennings." He turned to the woman. "If you'll follow me."

Ms. Jennings followed Elias through a door and down a hallway to an office in the back. As soon as they walked in Elias closed the door, took Ms. Jennings by her hand, and started kissing her passionately. Ms. Jennings was tentative at first and then she responded with equal passion. After a few minutes she pulled away from Elias.

"Careful now. I can't let you ruffle me up too much. I have to go back to work."

"Damn Bianca! It's bad enough you have to work on a Saturday but do you have to be so uptight about it?"

"I'm not uptight. I always want to make a good impression. You never know who's looking at you."

"Yeah but still…"

"We can't all be like you. It would be nice to live in a world where I can wear a T-shirt and jeans to work."

"You can if you want. It called self-employment. You

should try it."

"I could not disappoint my mother like that. She worked hard for me to get to where I am now."

"What about what you want?" Elias asked

"What I want is your sexy ass." Bianca reached and pulled Elias to her and kissed him aggressively.

Elias pulled away from the kiss and smiled at Bianca. "Now I know I got you hot now. You said the A-word. What's next? 'Gosh darn?'" Elias grinned as he pushed Bianca to the edge of the desk in the office. Bianca sat on the edge of the desk and wrapped her legs around Elias.

"Stop making fun of me," Bianca pouted.

Elias began to rub Bianca's thick and shapely calves. "I only say what I say because I love you."

Bianca unwrapped her legs from around Elias. "What did I tell you about that? What we have isn't about love. It's all about undercover fun."

"Yeah, undercover," Elias said while trying to keep his composure.

Bianca began to smooth out her dress skirt. "Please do not play around. You know my situation."

"Why not just leave the situation?"

"You know I will not leave Jeffrey. He's the type of man my mother has wanted for me all my life. Do you think I'm going to give that up?"

"No, guess not. We can't disappoint mother."

"No we can't. I know you understand." Bianca put her arms around Elias and gave him a deep kiss.

Elias gently broke the kiss. "Yes I do. When will I see you again?"

"Sometime next week. We'll get a hotel room and finish what we started."

"Sounds good to me. You ready to go?"

Bianca smoothed out her skirt one more time. "How do I look?"

"You look beautiful as always."

"Thank you."

Elias and Bianca left the office and walked to the entrance of the store.

"Thank you Ms. Jennings for your time," Elias said as he shook Bianca's hand in a business-like fashion.

Bianca had an expressionless demeanor. "And yours as well. I look forward to doing business with you in the future,"

Elias watched Bianca walk away and then returned to the back office. After Elias disappeared one of the young sales clerks turned to her co-worker. "Gurllll, who he think he fooling?"

Once in his back office Elias locked the door behind him and went to a refrigerator to get out a beer. He opened it and sat down taking a sip as tears began to well up in his eyes.

****

Bianca admired herself in the full-length mirror in the master bedroom of her luxury condo in Arlington, Virginia. Her black designer gown fitted like a second skin. She liked the feel of the dress against her healthy body. Her hair was well done and her make-up was expertly applied. She smiled as she looked at her size fourteen body. Bianca remembered when she was younger how she wanted to be a model. She also remembered her mother's words: *Chile, you're too big to be a model. A woman looking like you can only be a professional. Don't go for pipe dreams.*

So here I am, Bianca thought. She was an executive with a local bank. She had everything her mother wanted for her: the status, the condo, the luxury car, and the top credit rating. Unlike other professional Black women she also had a man on her level, Jeffery Tyler.

Jeffery was the owner of Tyler Enterprises, a multi-million dollar company specializing in property management. Jeffery was a man straight out of a romance novel. The kind of man her mother wanted for her. He was light-skinned first of all, because according to her mother, "those dark-skinned African looking low-lifes weren't smart enough." Bianca wondered if she and her mother, Wanda, were smart enough since they were dark-complexioned.

Jeffery was also 6'2", muscular with light eyes and good hair as Wanda called it. When Wanda first met Jeffery she decided that he was indeed perfect for her daughter. Indeed Jeffery was just perfect. Too perfect in fact.

Bianca was lost in thought as the doorbell rang.

"Good evening Jeffery," Bianca said as she opened the door.

"Good evening to you my love," Jeffery said as he walked in and gave Bianca a kiss on her cheek.

"My you look handsome as always," Bianca said as she looked at Jeffery in his black suit.

"Are you ready?"

"Yes I am, I've been looking forward to this evening for a long time."

"Well then, the Mercedes awaits."

****

Bianca kept her smile as she listened to the conversations of the men and women around the table as they talked about stock portfolios, corporate diversity, and played the standard game at Black Bourgeois gatherings: Negro Geography. Bianca smiled as the people around her discussed their schools, their fraternities and sororities, and most importantly their professions as they handed one another business cards trumpeting their positions in the corporate world.

One thing Bianca liked about Jeffery was that he didn't play Negro Geography. In fact he said very little about his past, even to her. Overall the evening wasn't that bad. They were at a charity fundraiser featuring a world renowned piano player, Leon Patrick. His performance was proceeded by a dinner. Bianca enjoyed the dinner and listened to the conversations of the people at the table. One of the men, named Sinclair Pennington, was particularly annoying. He was talking about a friend of his who was involved with someone he termed a "ghetto chick."

"I mean this broad is a walking billboard for tackiness," Sinclair said. He was light-skinned with a pudgy face and body. He was the president of a division at a local cable company.

"Was she that bad?" Michelle, Sinclair's date for the evening asked. She was the same complexion as Sinclair but had a slim petite built which contrasted sharply with Sinclair's dough-like body.

"She had the worst weave I've ever seen. She had no class. She would come to an event like this wearing a cut-off shirt and leggings showing her too big butt. On top of that she's dark-skinned."

Sinclair, oblivious to Bianca stiffening across the table continued. "I can't believe Bradley got caught up with such trash. He's from a good family, went to Morehouse and then business school at Penn. I still can't believe he took up with a ghetto chick."

"Must be what he likes," Jeffery said. "She must have some redeeming qualities."

"Please," Sinclair said, warming to the subject. "People like her do not belong with people like us."

"Who are people like us?" Jeffery asked.

"Who're you're kidding, Jeff? We're the cream of the crop. The talented tenth. The best Black America has to offer. We all have the same background. You know what I'm talking about Jeff."

"Yeah I do. But I don't think we should look down on those who are less fortunate or haven't been blessed with the same advantages. Sinclair you spoke of the Talented Tenth. Wasn't the purpose of the Talented Tenth to lead the Black community? To lead, means that we have to interact with the rest of the community."

"Look Jeff, I believe in charity and our responsibility to 'the people' but do we need to sleep with them? I don't think so," Sinclair said.

"I think we shouldn't be so harsh," Jeffery said.

"They're not us. Those ghetto dwellers hold us back. I hate when one of my white co-workers talk about some rapper like those thugs represent Black America."

"Apparently we're the true representatives of Black people," Bianca said, breaking her silence.

"Yes we are," Sinclair said noting that Bianca was the darkest woman at the table and one of the darkest in the room. She was also one of the heaviest in the room. He wondered about Bianca's background.

"The recital's about to begin," Michelle said.

The rest of the evening was spent listening to the concert pianist as Bianca's face remained a stoic mask.

****

"Did you enjoy the evening?" Jeffery asked as he stood outside the door of Bianca's condo.

"I certainly did Jeffery. Notwithstanding your friend, Sinclair," Bianca responded.

"Don't worry about that asshole. And he's not my buddy. I hope he didn't say anything to make you feel uncomfortable."

"He's just saying what he feels."

"You're a kind person. Well it was a great evening. I look forward to seeing you next week."

"Would you like to come in?" Bianca asked, already knowing the answer.

"You know I can't do that."

25

"Yes I do," Bianca said, while masking her disappointment.

"I don't want to start something we can't finish," Jeffery said.

"You're right. Good night Jeffery."

"Goodnight Bianca," Jeffery said as he gave her a kiss on her cheek and watched her walk into her apartment. Jeffery walked to his car thinking that Bianca was a good woman. Not at all like Sharon.

Chapter 3

Jeffery glared at the man in front of him, Joshua Miller. "This website is crap." Joshua designed the website for Tyler Enterprises.

"How can you say it's crap? It's one of my best works," Joshua responded nervously. He sat on the other side of the desk in Jeffery's spacious office.

"If it is, I hate to see your other sites." Jeffery's stare was intense.

"W-What is the problem?" Joshua tried to maintain his

composure. He was told that Jeffery, despite his pretty boy looks, could be very intimidating.

"The problem? Where do I start? First of all, the website is ugly. It doesn't look good period. Then half the links are broken and you're supposed to keep the content updated. I'm paying you to handle this. I shouldn't have to keep track of your job."

"You don't. I'm perfectly capable of doing my job. Nobody else has a problem with my work."

"I'm not everybody else. I demand the best. If you can't do this the right way I can find somebody else."

Joshua's nervousness began to turn to anger. "What do you want? Nobody else has a problem with the site. I don't need to deal with this."

"I don't like the tone of your voice. I'm going to exercise the escape clause on your contract and let you go."

"Let me go!?!" Joshua's anger began to rise. "I don't need your contract! I got other clients who appreciate my work! If you don't like my shit then fuck your yellow ass then."

"Leave my office and this building. Despite that bullshit site you provided you'll get your money. But make no mistake." Jeffery measured his words carefully. "If you ever speak to me like that again I'll not only hurt you financially but I'll take to the streets if necessary."

Joshua's boldness left him. "P-Perfectly."

After Joshua left, Jeffery was angry with himself for not showing more self-control. Even after all these years he still needed to control his emotions better. He got up from his desk and went to the private restroom in his office. He looked at himself in the mirror as he took a damp towel to his face and then made sure his shirt and tie were straight. He hated losing his cool and he needed to make sure everything was still in place.

He went back to his desk to read over the progress reports for all of his businesses. Tyler Enterprises focused on two primary areas: property management and retail stores. Jeffery's company owned several strip malls, office buildings, apartment buildings, and single family homes in an area stretching from Philadelphia to Richmond. Not bad for somebody who had just recently turned thirty-three. As if the properties weren't enough, Jeffery owned a chain of urban apparel stores. Jeffery had everything he wanted in life including the most precious thing: control. Every aspect of his life was in order. His business was thriving. Bianca was the perfect woman. Everything was perfect. Well except for one thing: Jeffery needed a new website designer.

Jeffery didn't want to rely on another recommendation. He would design the site himself if he had the time to learn website design. Since he didn't have the time he decided to find a designer on his own.

Jeffery had been searching the net for maybe an hour when he came across the website for Code Designs. He liked what he saw. Jeffery found a contact number for the owner of the company, Danny Code, and dialed immediately.

"Good afternoon, thank you for calling Code Designs. Danny Code speaking. How may I be of service?"

Jeffery was already impressed with Danny's professionalism. "Hello Mr. Code. This is Jeffery Tyler of Tyler Enterprises. I visited your website and I'm impressed with your work. I would like to meet with you to discuss Code Designs revamping my company's website."

This brotha is right to the point, Danny thought as he responded. "I'm honored that *the* Jeffery Tyler contacted me himself."

"You've heard of me?" Jeffery asked. Despite the size of his business he kept a relatively low profile.

"Anybody who's serious about building a business has heard about you, especially somebody into clothes. I've shopped at a couple of your stores."

"I'm honored then."

"I'm surprised you would call me yourself. Don't you have assistants to take care of things like this for you?"

"I do for the most part. I still have to micro-manage. Some people need someone to check their every move."

"So somebody else was supposed to call me but didn't?"

"Not at all. This was just something I felt I needed to take care of myself. I have trouble getting the type of website I want."

"I get you."

"What does your schedule look like for next week?"

"I'm free anytime. I make my own schedule."

"Let's meet on Tuesday. Do you know where the Schuyler building is downtown?"

"Yeah I do. I heard it's a nice building. How's having an office there?"

"I own the building."

"My bad."

"Don't worry about it. Let's meet at 11:00 am."

"Okay that'll work."

"Bring a portfolio. I have a feeling your best work isn't on the net."

"You're right about that."

"I look forward to meeting you."

"Me too. Peace.

"Good bye," Jeffery said as hung up the phone. Now that the website was taken care of everything was back in order.

As it should be.

****

"So I have a meeting with Jeffery Tyler on Tuesday," Danny said to Yumi as he parked his car. Danny and Yumi were going to one of the hottest clubs in town, *Erotique.* Danny had on a white long sleeve muscle shirt while Yumi had on a midriff shirt and a black spandex mini skirt.

"I'm very proud of you Danny," Yumi said as she got out of Danny's Mustang.

Danny locked his car door and walked around the car to Yumi's side. "In or out of bed?"

"You are so…sexual. I mean your work as an artist."

"Well I am skilled in the art of love."

"Yes Danny, you are. I'm serious, you are one of the best I've seen. I know you're going places."

"Thanks, that's always good to hear," Danny smiled.

"You have a pretty smile," Yumi beamed. "I'm ready to dance."

Rom Wills

"Are you really? I'll try not to hurt you," Danny said as they reached the end of the line for the club.

After fifteen minutes Danny and Yumi made it into the club. Wasting little time they went to the dance floor. They began to dance in sync to their own rhythm. Danny was in another world as he soaked in the sensuous energy coming off of Yumi. Their erotic dance was drawing the attention of the people in the club. Danny was the object of both envy and admiration from the Black men in the club as they looked at Yumi with lust filled eyes. Danny was oblivious to their attention. The Black women in the club were another matter. They stared with malice at Danny and Yumi. Danny, because they felt personally rejected by a fine Black man. Yumi, because she had stolen one of their precious few men. Unlike Danny, Yumi noticed the attention she received and responded by dancing even more erotically with Danny. Yumi turned around and bent lightly to allow Danny to grind her in a manner that would only be more intimate if they were both naked.

The grinding started on the dance floor continued at Yumi's apartment as she moaned rhythmically with her head buried in her pillow, and her butt in the air as Danny in a balance of power and tenderness pushed forward while pulling Yumi to him. The intensity increased as Yumi began to yell in Japanese until she climaxed. Yumi's several contractions triggered Danny's release as he trembled uncontrollably and collapsed onto the bed.

They both laid in an embrace for nearly ten minutes before Yumi gained enough strength to speak.

"I love y…having sex with you." Yumi rubbed Danny's brow.

Danny was breathing hard. "You don't love me you love my doggy-style,"

"You are so funny," Yumi said sarcastically. "This is the first time you've been this tired after sex."

"You wore me out on the dance floor Yumi-chan. Did you have a good time tonight?"

"I had a great time tonight especially getting all those jealous stares from the women in there."

"People were staring? How come I didn't notice?"

"Danny you're kidding? You didn't notice all the people looking at us? We were the center of attention."

"They were probably paying more attention to you. They wouldn't look my way if you weren't there. Black women don't look at me."

"I don't know what gave you that idea. We're always getting angry looks from Black women."

"Ah they're just looking because we're different races. They wouldn't notice me if I was walking down the street by myself."

"I don't believe that from what I've seen. Why are you so hard on Black women?"

"They're hard on me. They really don't care about me."

"Have you gone out with a Black woman before?"

Danny looked away from Yumi for a brief second. "No...I haven't."

"How come?"

"Just haven't. I really don't feel like talking about it," Danny said with a ting of anger.

"Okay Danny. I won't press the issue. Just don't be so

hard on the sistas."

"Funny for you to say that."

"I know I'm not Black but with the angry stares I also see looks of sadness. I believe people should be more open-minded but that's not reality. I don't feel guilty about being with you but I know we will not always be together. You never know where you'll find happiness."

"You have a kind heart, Yumi-chan," Danny said as he put his arm around Yumi.

"So do you Danny if you allow it to shine."

Chapter 4

Danny walked through the mall oblivious to the women young and old whose stomachs fluttered as he headed for his destination, *Robbins Books*. He nodded to a man working at the counter and walked toward the religion and spirituality section. Danny continued to withdraw into his own world as he picked up a couple of books and sat down in one of the leather chairs in the store. He was so deep into one particular book he failed to notice that a recent acquaintance of his walked into the store and headed straight to the man at the counter.

"Hi Elias," Alicia said as she hugged Elias after he walked around the counter to greet her.

"Hi yourself. You're looking great as usual. Hot date?" Elias asked sarcastically as he viewed Alicia's T-shirt and sweats along with her pulled back hair and big glasses.

"Ha-ha, very funny. You should do comedy."

"Can't. The honeys in the audience would be too distracting. Besides they may make me dress up. I can't give this up." Elias waved his hand over his T-shirt and jeans.

"You always bring a smile to my face. My book come in yet?"

"Nah, not yet."

"Dang, I'm just going to have to browse today in my section."

"Yeah well you're going to have to share the space." Elias pointed to Danny who was still oblivious to everyone else in the store.

Alicia pulled Elias and stepped out of Danny's line of sight. "Oh God."

"What's wrong with you?"

"Do you know that man?" Alicia pointed to Danny as the butterflies began to form in her stomach.

"Not really, which is ironic since he comes in here all the time but never says anything. He'll go straight to the non-fiction section and stay for a couple of hours. Sometimes he won't buy anything. When he does buy something, he may spend close to a hundred dollars. Where do you know him from?"

36

"I met him at the club. He tipped me a twenty."

"That brotha? He don't look like he need to go to a nudie bar. No homo."

"You'd be surprised. Besides you go to 'nudie' bars as you so crudely put it, and you're no slouch in the looks department yourself."

"Now there you go," Elias sighed. "Are you going to go over and say hi?"

"I'm too shy."

"You? Shy? How much did you brag about making last month?"

"That's different. Steam…is different from Alicia. She's more outgoing and bold. I'm a bookworm."

"You think he's fine don't you?"

"Yes…but…"

"Then get your ass over there because there's been a couple of customers who have checked him out already. You better get yours."

"Okay. I'll try," Alicia said with a shy smile as she walked confidently over to Danny.

Elias shook his head. "She'll try, my ass. Have the nerve to be switching."

"Hello Stranger," Alicia said as she sat down in the chair next to Danny's.

"Hello…do I know you? Please don't take this as a pickup but I know I've seen you before but I can't think of where."

"You gave me twenty dollars a couple of weeks ago at

Riley's."

Danny cracked a rare smile. "Steam? Get out. How are you? You look different."

"I'm fine. By the way when I'm not working you can call me Alicia Green."

"Okay Alicia Green. So are you a reader Alicia Green? Bookstores are on one of my favorite places to hang out...Alicia Green."

"Another comedian," Alicia laughed. She liked Danny's smile. "To answer your question I do like to read. You should see my place. I have books stacked on top of books."

"What do you like to read?"

"I read just about everything, particularly books on yoga, holistic living, and different African and Asian religions."

"Beauty and brains. So what do you think about spirituality? Do you practice a particular faith?"

"That's interesting. Most people avoid discussions about spirituality. To answer your question I don't follow a particular path. I believe all religions are roads leading to the same destination, which is the God within."

"You're one of those people who believe that God is inside of us?"

"Yes I am. I know we are all a part of God. We don't have to pray to some outside force when everything we want is inside of us."

"Intriguing."

"Now that you've asked me...what path do you follow?"

"I don't. I guess you would call me an agnostic. I'm not

sure if there is a God. That's why I like going through these books. I have a pretty sizable collection myself. I focus more on history, philosophy and male-female relationships though."

"Really? I'll be interested in checking out your book collection. Back to the spirituality piece…have you found anything to convince you about God?"

"I've read some fascinating things but nothing has grabbed me yet."

"Take your time. You need to be comfortable with your path in life."

"That's a surprise. Usually somebody would have tried to convert me."

"It's my belief that we all have different missions in life. Maybe your mission requires you to be more in the world than in a church or temple."

"That's deep. You're very stimulating. Would you like to get something in the food court? My treat."

Alicia smiled. "I would love to."

"Let me put these books back." Danny took the books off the table and walked to the shelves to return them.

"I'll be over by the counter," Alicia said as she walked over to Elias. Danny joined her.

"Are you ready?" Danny asked.

"In a second." Alicia looked at Danny and Elias. "Do you two know each other?"

"No," Danny said as he extended his hand to Elias. "Danny Code."

"Elias Robbins," Elias said as he shook Danny's hand. "I'm

the owner of this fine store."

"You have a great place. I think very highly of it."

"I know you do. I see you in here all the time. I figured you'd speak at some point."

"Humph. I guess I'm in my own little world at times."

"That you are. Thanks for letting us visit," Elias laughed.

"Anytime," Danny grinned.

"Now have my little girl back at a decent time. Don't make me break out the shotgun."

"Yes sir. I'll be friendlier next time bro," Danny said.

"Yeah whatever. I'm hungry," Alicia said, pretending to be impatient.

"Well off we go. Nice meeting you Elias."

"You too, Danny."

Alicia grabbed Danny's hand and pulled him out of the store. "I really am hungry."

Bianca studied the couple walking towards her as she headed to *Robbins Books*. They looked great together. Now he's fine, Bianca thought, even though he's dark-skinned. Real pretty eyes. Bianca hated that Jeffery never wanted to hold her hands publicly. Maybe it was because of her complexion and her weight.

Bianca saw Elias immediately when she walked into the store.

"Hello Mr. Robbins. How are you today?' Bianca asked as she put up the usual front despite being the only person in the store besides Elias. The other workers were on break.

"I'm fine Ms. Jennings. Were we supposed to meet today?"

"Yes we had a meeting scheduled."

"Hmmm, it must have slipped my mind. Ummm, we need to reschedule. Despite the lull right now, we expect to be busy this evening with an author signing."

"Actually, we didn't have anything planned. I just thought you would be available. You always talk about being more spontaneous."

"There's a time and place for everything."

"I guess there is Mr. Robbins."

"Bianca, we're the only ones in here. Let's stop playing games."

"Mr. Ro...Elias, you know we have to be careful."

"How is Jeff?" Elias asked, barely masking his contempt.

"Same oh. Great businessman. Knows what's best for the world. Handsome. He's exactly what my mother would want," Bianca said distantly.

"You always say that. What do you want?"

"I want him...I think. Sometimes I don't know where my mother ends and I begin."

"Mothers are a trip aren't they?"

"Yes they are. You know, you have never talked about your mother."

"She's a character. Her and my sister."

"I remember you told me you still live with them."

"More like the other way around but yeah it's a trip."

"Why don't they get their own place?"

"For what? I pay all the bills around there anyway."

"Why don't they work?"

"That's complicated. Maybe I'll share with you one day. Right now I need to get back to work and plus my workers will be back any minute now."

"Yes you have a family to support," Bianca said snidely as she walked out without saying goodbye.

"Yeah a family to support," Elias said softly.

Chapter 5

Elias was having a good time at *Riley's* with his buddies, Jimmy and Mike. A couple of times a month Elias would get together with his old college friends. Jimmy was extremely overweight, tipping the scales at 300 pounds. His considerable girth belied the fact he was a stockbroker who made nearly a million dollars a year. Elias's other friend, Mike, was only about 5'3" and wiry. His stature belied the fact that he was an associate at a prestigious law firm. He was also quite a ladies' man.

Gathering at a strip club was a ritual that began during their days as undergraduates at American University in DC.

The men watched the women dance one by one until it was time for Steam to come to the stage. As usual the men went crazy, tipping her before she even finished undressing. Jimmy was one of the first men to get up as he walked over and slowly and meticulously tipped Steam ten dollars in ones.

As Steam got more into her dance her movements stroked the erotic fires in the men in the club. The vast majority of the men tipped Steam as her movements seemed to release the hold the men had on their wallets. Jimmy was moved to give Steam even more money.

After her set and counting her tips quickly, Steam put on a halter top and a pair of booty shorts and walked out to greet the customers. Her last stop was the table with Elias and his friends.

"Hey baby! Thanks for coming out!" Steam gave Elias an affectionate hug.

Elias looked Steam up and down. "You know I had to check you out girl! Fine as you're looking I don't know about this platonic thing. Steam, these are my boyz from college. You've already met Jimmy."

"You are so beautiful," Jimmy said as he took Steam's hand. He was at a loss for words.

"Hey Jimmy, here's something to wipe the drool from your mouth," Elias joked as he handed his friend a napkin.

Jimmy finally let go of Steam's hand. "Man why you always joking?"

"Hello Steam, my name is Mike Harper. Your performance was wonderful," Mike said suavely. "Please join us for a drink."

"I can sit down for a minute," Steam said. "I don't drink though."

"Fair enough." Mike pulled out a seat for Steam.

"How's the night been going for you," Elias asked.

"It's been pretty good. The men here have been showing a lot of love. Isn't that right Jimmy?"

"Y-you are so beautiful," Jimmy said nervously.

"Man can work a business deal but gets nervous around a beautiful woman," Elias laughed.

"Elias leave him alone." Steam turned to Jimmy. "Calm down baby. Believe it or not I'm shy myself sometimes."

"I find that hard to believe," Jimmy responded.

"You'd be surprised," Steam said as she rubbed Jimmy's arm.

"That makes me feel better," Jimmy smiled.

"Hey I'm shy too," Elias teased.

"Always the comedian," Steam said. "Gentlemen, I need to get ready for my net set. I'll talk to y'all later."

"Nice meeting you," Mike said.

"I look forward to your next dance," Jimmy said.

"Go shake your money maker," Elias said.

Steam smiled at Elias's comment as she walked to the dressing room. Her thoughts were interrupted by a man's voice.

"Hey boo. You still don't holla at me." The voice belonged to Han.

"You still don't tip me," Steam said as she walked past Han.

"I don't have to tip freak." Han reached out and palmed Steam's butt.

That's when all hell broke loose.

Steam turned around immediately and delivered two roundhouse kicks to Han's ribs. Despite the pain, Han lunged at Steam. Steam stepped slightly to the side and delivered an elbow to Han's face causing him to fall to the ground with blood on his face. By this time the bouncers had rushed over and grabbed Han before Steam could hurt him further.

The whole scene astonished Jimmy while Elias and Mike were calm and collected.

"Y'all see that! She kicked his ass!" Jimmy yelled.

"That happens in places like this. Don't be surprised though about Steam. She has studied Thai boxing as well as some other shit."

"No biggie, part of the show as far as I'm concerned," Mike said, suave as ever.

"You two crack me up." Jimmy shook his head.

****

Steam got home about four in the morning and fell out on her bed. As she drifted off to sleep she began to dream. She was a young girl playing in her house when she walked past a man sitting on a couch watching TV. The man commented on her adolescent body. He said she was going to have a nice booty when she grew up. The man's hand reached out, palming her butt…

Steam woke up in a sweat as she realized that the incident with Han had brought up an unpleasant memory.

Chapter 6

Danny sat calmly in Jeffery Tyler's office as his portfolio was being reviewed. Outwardly Danny's face was an impassive mask. Inwardly, Danny was astonished that the owner of Tyler Enterprises would interview him personally. After a few minutes Jeffery looked up from the portfolio with a smile on his face.

"I'm very impressed with both your portfolio and the websites that you have designed for other companies."

Danny nodded. "Thank you. I really appreciate that."

"I'm really impressed with how you use flash to grab attention on the webpage. It's very enticing. That's what I'm looking for. First impressions mean a great deal in business. I want visitors to the site to be impressed. I want them to bookmark the site and be ready to run out to one of my stores. Reviewing your work I know you can do that."

"Thank you. If I design a website that doesn't increase your bottom line I'm not doing my job right."

"Now that's what I want to hear. I'll have someone from the accounting department write up a contract for you and have the office manager set up an office for you."

"Set up an office for me?" Danny looked at Jeffery intently.

"Yes, where else would you work?" Jeffery had a surprised look on his face.

"I work from my home."

"Anybody who works for me needs to be where I can check in on them."

Danny kept his cool. "I don't need someone to check in on me. I'm not some intern who's going to surf the net on the job."

"I'm not saying that. I need to be in a position where I know what's going with people working for me regardless of whether they are employees or contractors. I don't make exceptions."

"You'll need to in this case. I don't need to be micro-managed. If you need to contact me I can be reached by phone or e-mail."

Jeffery barely kept his composure. "If I'm paying

somebody to work for me I have the right to have my say in their work."

"You'll have it in this case. I just won't be in an office in this building."

"Apparently you don't want this contract then." Jeffery struggled to keep his anger down.

"Not under the conditions you're offering. I work my way or no way. I'm my own man," Danny said with steel in his voice and a piercing glare.

Jeffery blinked for a second as Danny's eyes communicated an uncompromising message. "You're not going to back down are you?"

Danny observed Jeffery's reaction but kept his composure. "I'm my own man. I worked hard to create the life I wanted to live. I live on my terms and no one else's. If it means I don't get this contract so be it. Just like you found my website other people will as well. Money is very important but not as important as a man's dignity."

I'm my own man, Jeffery thought as he contemplated Danny's statements. "I want you to meet with the financial officer on the way out. I'm also going to increase my offer by 20 percent. You can work from wherever you please."

Danny was surprised. "Why are you going sign me up? Especially after what I just said."

"You were willing to walk away from a lot of money because of your principles. Excuse the expression but you're weren't willing to be a hoe. Too many men in this society sell their soul to the highest bidder. They willingly take it up the ass for the right amount of money. How can I respect a man who will give away their manhood so easily? I see you're not a man to give up his manhood. Neither am I. If I was in your position I would have said the exact same thing. Hell, you were calmer about it than I would have been. It's rare I encounter a man like you. I would be honored to have you design my website." Jeffery stood up to offer Danny his hand.

Danny stood up and shook Jeffery's hand. "I'd be honored to provide my services to you."

Jeffery walked around his desk. "The financial officer's office is right down the hall. Ms. Walters will take care of you." Jeffery held the door for Danny.

"I'll have something for your review in a few days. I already have some ideas. Have a good afternoon," Danny said as he walked out the door.

"You do as well. I look forward to your work."

Jeffery closed the door behind Danny and sat down at his desk.

I'm my own man, Jeffery thought as he leaned back in his chair. He closed his eyes and his mind drifted back to when he was five years old. His father was packing his clothes while arguing with his mother. His parents had a volatile relationship with each trying to struggle for control. As a child, Jeffery wondered what his parents saw in each other. His father was a fiercely independent man while his mother was a manipulator. It seemed that his mother's mission in life was to break the will of his father. His father was known for his strong will as he had never worked for anyone a day in his life. His father was a contractor who fixed up houses and even owned a few. His father, Eddie Tyler, took crap off of no one and would turn down jobs if a client was disrespectful in anyway. *I'm my own man*, Eddie Tyler would say every day. It was his constant mantra. His philosophy of life.

Perhaps it was the challenge of breaking a strong man which drew Jeffery's mother to his father. He knew many women wanted a challenge in a man. What could be more of a challenge than a strong willed man? Even the strongest man could only take so much. After an argument, Eddie started packing his clothes and walked out of the house. His parents would divorce a year later. Eddie died when Jeffery was a teenager as years of hard work took their toll on the body of his father. Eddie's funeral was the last time Jeffery cried.

Jeffery was brought back to the present by the phone ringing.

"This is Jeffery Tyler."

"Hi Jeff. Are we still on for lunch?" The voice belonged to Bianca.

"Of course we are. I've never stood you up before have I?"

"No you haven't. I don't take things for granted."

"You can with me. My word is always good. I'll drive by to pick you up in twenty minutes.

"I look forward to seeing you.

****

"Thank you for the lunch," Bianca said as she and Jeff

walked back to his car. They were on 13th street in downtown DC.

"My pleasure as always. It seems like you're getting a lot of attention." Jeffery noticed several men turning their necks to look at Bianca who looked very sexy in her business suit.

Bianca blushed. "These men check out anything in a skirt."

"I wish they wouldn't be so blatant about it. You are walking with a man."

"You know men in DC don't care."

"They need to care when I'm with you."

Jeffery and Bianca were making small talk as they walked when a voice called out to Bianca. "Damn Ma! You look um, um good! Can you give a brotha a taste? Lawd!!! Forget that bamma you with. He can't do you like I can."

Jeffery and Bianca looked and saw a man with unkempt clothes and dirty skin.

Jeffery glared at the man.

The man became belligerent. "Who the fuck you looking at you light ass nigga!"

Jeffery looked at the man and despite having on a business suit moved swiftly, grabbing the man by neck and slamming him against the wall of the building the man was next to.

"I'm looking at you." Jeffery's voice was cold and mean. "Don't you know not to fuck with a light ass nigga 'cause we crazy? I'll break my foot off in your muthafucking ass out here you little broke bitch. Don't ever disrespect a lady like that."

"I-I'm just playing. I-I don't mean any... anything." The

man was scared out of his wits.

"Jeff, let him go. He didn't bother me really. He's not worth it," Bianca said while conscious of the crowd they were drawing around them.

"You better pray I don't run into you where there are no witnesses." Jeffery let the man go and backed away from slowly.

Jeffery and Bianca didn't say anything until they were in Jeffery's car. Bianca could no longer keep her silence no longer.

"Jeffery, was that necessary?"

"Sometimes you have to let people how far you're willing to go for respect."

"I understand but in front of people like that? What if somebody recognized you?"

"They'll know not to mess with Jeffery Tyler."

"Jeffery, you're the head of a multi-million dollar corporation. You can't lower yourself to the level of these street dwellers. I know that wasn't how you were raised."

"Frankly Bianca you really don't know how I was raised. I don't care to discuss this anymore."

"Ok fine we will not discuss this anymore."

Jeffery and Bianca were silent and lost in their thoughts for the rest of the drive.

Chapter 7

Danny felt good. After his meeting with Jeffery Tyler, Danny had lunch at a downtown DC restaurant which had a buffet. After lunch he walked around taking in the energy of the women going to and from their offices during their lunch breaks. It was so intoxicating seeing women of all races in their sexy strides, especially the sistas. They came in all shapes and sizes and colors from light enough to pass to the deepest darkest chocolate. Too bad none of these beautiful Black women would ever want him, Danny thought.

Danny was lost in thought as a voice called out to him.

"Do you have spare change for the homeless?"

"I'm sorry I…"Danny turned to the voice and saw a young woman with her left arm around a young boy. Both were wearing dirty clothes and looked like they hadn't washed in days. Danny peered into the eyes of the boy and saw a familiar gaze. Danny thought back to his childhood. He had a really strong memory of when he was eight years old. He was digging through a trash can when an older man stopped him. The man asked him why he was digging in the trash. Danny said he was hungry. The man shook his head, got out his wallet and handed Danny a five dollar bill.

"Are you okay sir?" The woman's voice brought Danny back to the present.

"Uh…yeah." Danny reached into his wallet and pulled out several twenties. "Here's one hundred dollars. Hopefully this will hold you over for a little while."

The woman took the money. "Oh thank you sir. Thank you! God bless you!" The woman turned to the boy next to her. "Baby we can get something to eat!"

Danny saw the smile on the boy's face and felt good. The boy reminded him of himself at the same age.

"Why did you give me so much money? Most people would have given a dollar at most. You…don't want anything…do you?" The woman began to look apprehensive.

Danny shook his head. "It's not like that. It's just that I've been where you are. The money is a gift. I don't want anything in return. No I take that back. I do want something in return."

The women stiffened. "What do you want?"

"I want you to always love your little boy."

"That's it? I do that anyway." The woman put a loving arm around the boy and pulled him closer.

"Just never stop. Have a nice day." Danny turned and began to walk away.

"God bless you sir!" the woman yelled.

What kind of God would allow people to be on the street like that, Danny thought as he continued to walk down the street.

****

Danny received two texts as he walked into his apartment. The texts came from Yumi and Alicia. Danny called Yumi first.

"Hello Danny," Yumi answered on the second ring.

"Hi Yumi. I got your text. What's going on with you?"

"I'm studying for exams. I wanted to see what you were doing."

"Nothing much. Do you want me to come over?"

"As tempting as that sounds I have to study. Maybe we can get together Saturday night."

"That sounds good. So it's almost time for you to go back home huh. Seems like we just met."

"Yes it does." Yumi thought back to when she met Danny a few months ago at a gym. She first noticed Danny on an exercise bike every time she came to work out. She thought he was attractive when she first saw him but that was most of the men in the gym. What drew her to him was that Danny would work out and leave. Unlike most of the other men in the gym Danny wasn't looking to get his Mack on. Danny didn't say anything to her the first time she rode the exercise bike next to him. That would change in the next couple of weeks.

"I'm going to miss you, Yumi. Before you go let's make our last time together memorable."

"Let's do that. I have to get back to my studies. I'll give you a call in a couple of days, Danny. Bye-bye."

"Later." Danny put his phone down and then took his suit off and stretched out on his bed to take a nap.

Danny woke up hours later. His energy felt low. He also hadn't returned Alicia's text. He figured he would kill two birds with one stone.

****

The music was pumping at *Riley's Place* and the men were having a good time as always. Danny walked in and looked for a table to sit down at. He looked around until he saw a familiar face at a table by himself.

"What's up Elias," Danny said upon reaching the table. "Anybody sitting here?"

"Just me. Have a seat bruh."

Danny sat down. "How did you manage to keep a table for yourself?"

"I dunno. Maybe I'm giving off that Joe Ruffneck vibe," Elias laughed.

"Whatever works. When is Steam coming up? She invited me out tonight."

"She's been on already. The brothas didn't go as wild as they usually do, especially after last week."

Danny looked at Elias. "What are you talking about?"

"Mannn, Steam had to get raw with a brotha last week. This big ass, cornbread eating bamma grabbed Steam's butt and she got Kung Fu violent on his ass."

"Is she okay?"

"You mean is he okay. Steam knows some martial arts. She's not a black belt or anything but she can probably break a spine or two."

Danny chuckled. "I better watch myself with her."

"Yeah boy, I still got my shotgun." Elias sounded like an old man.

"Yes sir," Danny grinned.

As if on cue Steam came to the stage wearing pumps and a tight red spandex mini dress. As usual the men were lined up before she started taking off her clothes.

Steam did her routine, dancing in her own world as she was oblivious to the men around her. She only left her world long enough to acknowledge Elias and Danny before continuing her sensuous dance.

After her set, Steam emerged from backstage and thanked everyone who tipped her and headed over to Elias and Danny. Steam gave Danny a very warm and affectionate hug and kiss on his cheek.

"Hi baby!" Steam had her arms around Danny's neck and

was looking into his eyes. "You must have got my text. I'm so happy you came."

"I'm glad you invited me." Danny had his hands around Steam's waist.

"Get a room!" Elias snickered.

Steam let go of Danny and reached over to hug Elias.

"Don't be hugging me now. You've been all over another man," Elias said.

Steam sat down. "Ah baby, you still my boo."

"Yeah, yeah."

"You were great tonight." Danny slipped a twenty dollar bill into Steam's garter.

"I'm glad you loved it."

"I did and all the men in here."

"Whatever. I don't care about anybody in here, except for you two."

"I'm honored," Danny said.

"I meant it when I said to get a room," Elias interrupted.

Steam smiled. "Don't be jealous baby."

"Um hmm. Don't try to sweet talk me. I'm going to start giving Thunder more attention."

"She did say you were fine."

Elias looked surprised. "She did?"

"She always asks about you."

"Now that's a woman. Thunder puts those big legs around a brotha and it's all over."

"You want me to introduce y'all."

"Nah, an extra five dollars will do it."

Steam laughed. "You're trifling." She turned to Danny. "I really am glad you came out tonight. It means a lot to me."

"I bet you say that to all the guys."

"Just the ones with pretty eyes," Steam winked.

"I'm flattered."

"Hey you two," Elias said. "I'm about to get out of here. I have some things to do."

Steam stood up to give Elias a hug. "Thanks for coming out. I'll be by the store this week."

"Later man." Danny nodded to Elias.

Elias nodded to Danny. "You two have a good time."

"Where you headed baby?" Steam asked.

"I'm going to have my own good time."

Chapter 8

Elias hesitated at the apartment door. His alcohol induced courage was beginning to wear off. He knew he was taking a chance being there but after seeing Steam and Danny together he knew what he had to do. Elias took a deep breath, knocked on the door, and waited for a response. After a seeming eternity she responded from the other side of the door.

"Yes who is it?"

Elias responded nervously. "It's me Bianca. Elias."

Bianca cracked the door open slightly. "Elias! What are you doing here? How come you didn't call first? You can't come over like this. What if Jeffery was here?"

"Bianca, please let me in. You don't want your neighbors overhearing our conversation."

Bianca sighed and allowed Elias to enter her condo. "You didn't answer my questions."

"Dang, you ain't going to at least offer a brotha something to eat or drink." Elias sat down on a couch in the living room and leaned back.

Bianca sat down in an easy chair across from Elias. "I don't have time for your jokes. What the hell are you doing here!?!"

"Uh oh you said the H-word. I must really be in trouble," Elias laughed.

Bianca glared at Elias.

Elias sat upright in response and got serious. "I'm here to be with you. We haven't got together in a few weeks and really miss being with you. I had to see you tonight."

"Elias...Elias. I want to be with you too but you know the situation. You can't come over on a whim. You should've at least called first. That's just a matter of respect."

"You would have told me not to come."

"You're right I would have. What if Jeffery was over here? It would have been ugly."

"Who're your trying to fool? You told me Jeffery spends very little time over here."

"What if this was one of those times?"

"It's not like y'all would have been doing anything," Elias smirked. "You're the one who told me that he doesn't get affectionate with you. Shit, that's why I'm hitting it and he's not. At least that's what you told me."

"Elias please watch your language in my home." Bianca immediately thought back to when she first met Elias. She was at a woman's expo in at the Washington Convention Center, browsing through a book display when Elias approached her. Elias flirted with her like other men tried to but there was something different about his approach. Other men seemed like they wanted only sex while Elias seemed genuinely interested in getting to know her. Bianca surprised herself by giving Elias her work number thinking he wouldn't call anyway. Besides she was with Jeffery. Elias called her the next day and they had a great conversation. A few weeks later they would meet at a hotel several miles south of DC.

"I'm sorry," Elias said. "I'm frustrated we have to sneak around like this."

Bianca frowned. "I understand. I can't let Jeffery find out about us. He has such a temper. There's no telling what he might do."

"Or your mother," Elias remarked sarcastically.

"Please don't go there." Bianca hated when Elias mentioned her mother. "I'm going to have to ask you to leave." Bianca stood up and walked to the door.

Elias got the hint and lazily got off the couch. "It's too bad you have to live this way."

"What do you mean by that? I live very well."

"You have a domineering mother who's living life through you and a man who won't touch you. What kind of life is that?"

"Elias…please don't make this harder than it has to be." Bianca opened the condo door.

"You're the one making this hard." Elias hesitated and then leaned over to kiss Bianca on her lips. The kiss was cold and passionless.

"I'll talk to you later." Elias walked out the door as he struggled to keep his emotions in check.

"We'll see each other." Bianca closed and locked the door. She walked over to her couch and hugged herself as she stared into space.

****

Elias heard the music blasting as he pulled into his driveway. He sighed as he got out of his Ford Expedition and walked to the house. At this late hour his mother was still up and having a good time. Elias winced as he opened the door. The place was a mess as usual. All he asked his mother and sister to do was keep the place straight and they couldn't manage that one simple task.

Elias's thoughts were interrupted when he heard a man's voice come from the basement, one he didn't recognize. "Oh great she has a new friend."

Elias walked down the steps and saw his mother in a short dress on the couch and a man who looked like a reject from a 1970s pimp movie with his hands on her thigh. They were kissing passionately as Elias walked to the stereo system and turned off the power.

"Hey, what are you doing here Elias?" His mother pulled away from the man and straightened her dress.

"This is my house, Debbie. What kind of stupid question is that?"

"Hey boy! Watch your tone of voice with your mother!" The man stood up.

Elias looked at the man who was short, skinny, and had half his teeth missing while the four that remained were capped in gold. "Who the fuck are you? This is my house muthafucka. I pay the bills in here and not you. You don't know me. You better get your dusty ass out of here!"

"Elias don't talk to Eddie like that," Debbie pleaded. She sounded like a teenager who had been caught with a boy for the first time. "He's my guest."

"Yeah junior don't make me have to go upside your head." Eddie tried to sound tough.

Elias shoved Eddie so hard he fell over the coffee table.

"Okay, okay young blood.   It doesn't have to be this way." Eddie struggled to get to his feet. "I'll leave. I got too many other bitches for this." Eddie headed towards the steps.

"You don't have to leave," Debbie said as she followed Eddie up the steps and to the front door.

"I don't have to deal with this shit. I'm a pimp." Eddie tried to look cool.

"Your bamma ass ain't no pimp. Pimps got rides and I ain't seen no cars in front of the house when I pulled up. Get your ass out and don't step foot in my house again."

Eddie saw the malice in Elias's eyes and turned to Debbie before leaving. "I thought you were grown woman. Next time get your 'daddy's' permission before messing with any man."

Debbie was silent as the door closed behind Eddie. Elias broke the silence.

"Debbie I told you not to bring anymore strange men up in here. I damn near had to kill that last muthafucka who tried to move in here."

Debbie walked to the dining room and sat down at the table. "How come you don't let me have any fun? I want to have friends too."

"I don't have a problem with you having friends but why these dusty ass bammas you find in front of liquor stores?"

"They like me. Can I help it if they like me?" Debbie's voice was whinny.

"Those fools ain't trying to do shit with their lives. They see a big ol' house here and think they can move in. Damn Debbie why don't you think sometimes."

"Why won't you let your mother have some fun?" Tears began to well up in Debbie's eyes.

Elias let out a breath and put his hand on Debbie's shoulder. "Ma look. I want you to have a fulfilling life but dang can't you do it with some decent people. Here we are in one of the best neighborhoods in DC and you still act like you're over in the projects. I moved us out of there for a reason."

"I liked the people over there. You may have forgotten where you came from but I didn't. We have family over there."

"And they can stay over there for all I care." Elias sighed. "I know there was some good people over there but there were also the dregs of society as well. Human beings shouldn't have to live like some of those people did over there. I worked hard to get this house and have a place for you and Latisha. Where is she by the way?"

"She's out with Wayne."

"See that's what I'm talking about. All the men she could get with and she's with that two-bit hustler. They ain't bust him yet for those fake bags and watches?"

"Wayne's just trying to survive just like any other man. Your father was hustling the same way. Just like you."

"I'm not a hustler."

Debbie looked Elias squarely in the eye. "You're not a hustler? Oh you're selling books and real CD's now but I remember the days you were out on the streets trying to sell t-shirts and other cheap shit. You didn't think all of that stuff was real did you?"

Elias glared at Debbie.

"I don't know what you're getting mad about baby boy. You were good at the game. You made me so proud. My little man got the best grades in school and was the best little hustler in the streets. My little man wasn't afraid to work. Even when you went to American University you had your hustles going. Just like your father did before he was killed."

"Debbie I don't want to think about it," Elias said sadly.

"I know baby boy. Your father was a good man. He took care of us just like you do now. I know that's why you always run these niggas away from me. I'm grown though sweetheart. You gotta let your momma have some fun."

"Yeah Debbie. I want you to be with somebody but can you at least get with somebody with some class?"

"Your momma's getting older and set in her ways. I don't have a fancy degree or a business like you do. I don't have any skills. I'd be on welfare without you around."

"Debbie you can change. Please try. I'm going to bed. Good night." Elias got up walked to his room.

When Elias reached his room he saw the picture of his father, John, on his dresser. He picked up the frame. John Robbins was a hustler. Whether it was pool or craps or selling stolen goods John did what he had to do every day to survive. John eventually graduated to selling weed to make a little money. It was during a drug deal gone bad that John was killed. Though Elias was only ten at the time he realized that John's weakness was that he never really wanted to improve his circumstances. Elias wouldn't make that mistake. Elias became determined to leave that neighborhood and do something with life so he began hitting the books even harder than he had been and he started selling t-shirts for an older vendor in the neighborhood. He wasn't going to suffer his father's fate.

Elias put the picture back on his dresser and sat down on his bed. He thought about his mother's reaction to John's death. Within weeks of John's death, different men would come to the apartment to visit his mother. It seemed like these men were the lowest in the neighborhood. Debbie Robbins was one of those women who never quite grew up. The type who at fifty would try to hang out with teenagers.   Elias was forced to grow up before his time.

Elias laid back on his bed as thought about what his life may been like if he had a childhood.

Chapter 9

"Mother, where are you?" Bianca let herself into her mother's apartment while carrying several grocery bags. She turned her nose up as she looked around the messy apartment.

"Is that you Bianca?" The voice came from the bedroom.

"Yes mother, who else would it be?" Bianca walked to the kitchen with grocery bags. "I bought some food for you. I'll put it away for you."

"I'll be right out."

"Take your time mother. There's no rush." Bianca finished

putting the food away and walked out to the living room and leaned back on a couch.

"Bianca sit up please. That is no way to sit." Bianca's mother, Wanda, walked out of the bedroom wearing an old brown and dingy bathrobe. "You're slumming today aren't you?"

As Bianca sat up she looked down at the sweat shirt, jeans, and sneakers she was wearing. "I can't dress up every day. It is Saturday mother. This is the first time in a while I haven't had to work. I do need to relax sometimes."

Wanda sat down on the couch next to Bianca. "You always have to look your best. Even in situations you think are casual."

"I know mother. You have drummed that into my head since I was little." Bianca looked at her mother's disheveled appearance and thought that she may be looking into her own future. Even though Wanda was only in her late forties, she looked like someone in their sixties. Bianca often wondered if she would age as poorly.

"Maybe it's okay to slip up slip every now and then," Wanda said sadly.

Bianca noticed her mother's depressed mood. "I'll dress up the way I know I should next time I come over."

Wanda smiled. "Thanks that will make me feel good."

"What are you doing today?" Bianca decided to change the subject.

"There's nothing for me to do."

"Mother, why don't you go out? Don't you hate sitting around the apartment all day?"

"Where am I going? I don't have a job. I don't have a man,

71

and I don't have any friends. All I have is you."

"Yes mother I know. No one is stopping you from going out and making friends. What if I'm not around? What would you do then?"

"I would die if you weren't around."

Bianca sighed. "Mother, you could get along without me."

"Bianca, I put so much of my life into raising you. I don't have anything left." Wanda's thoughts wandered back to just before Bianca was born.

Wanda Jennings had been a star student in high school. Everyone agreed that she was headed someplace special. That is until she met Bobby Harris. Bobby was the most popular boy in school with his light-brown skin, muscular body, and wavy hair. He was also a star on the football team. All the girls vied for his attention including Wanda. Wanda felt special when Bobby spoke to her in the cafeteria the first time. Usually the boys ignored her because she was dark-skinned. Bobby made her feel special the next few weeks. So special it didn't take much for Wanda to give her virginity to Bobby.

The first time felt so good. Wanda felt beautiful for the first time in her life. She had sex with him a few more times. She felt he was the one until he began to see her less frequently. Then abruptly Bobby decided he didn't want to see Wanda anymore as Tonya, a slim light-skinned girl made herself available to Bobby. Wanda cried for a week and things took a turn for the worse when she realized her period was late.

Bianca brought Wanda back to the present. "Mother, I know you sacrificed so much to provide for me. That's why I work so hard to take care of you."

"You're made me so proud," Wanda smiled. "Do you have plans with Jeffery tonight?"

"Yes we will be attending a concert at the Kennedy Center."

"The Kennedy Center? That's so wonderful. You remember when I took you to all of those free concerts when you were little?"

Bianca winced slightly, unnoticed by her mother. "How can I forget? Those were memorable experiences."

"Are you looking forward to tonight? Jeffery is a wonderful man. He's perfect for you."

"Of course he is mother." Bianca looked around the apartment. "Mother sit down and relax for a little while. I'm going to straighten up a bit."

"You're such a perfect daughter. I don't know what I would do without you."

Bianca smiled pleasantly as she stood up from the couch. "Yes mother I know."

****

"Hello Elias," Bianca said as she walked into *Robbins Books*.

"Hello Ms. Je...you called me by my first name." Elias was surprised. He pulled Bianca to the side and spoke in a low voice. "I thought you were so concerned with appearances. What would your mother and Jeffery think?"

"I just saw my mother so don't mention her to me. Please don't fake like you care about Jeff."

73

"Okay I understand. To what do I owe the pleasure of this visit?"

"I want you. Badly!"

"Let's go back to my office."

"No not here. Let's be adventurous. You keep telling me to be more daring. Why don't you get your truck and follow me to a little park I know about."

"That'll work. Where are you parked at?"

"I'm in the Northside lot."

Elias thought for a second. "Walk out first and I'll follow in twenty minutes. We don't want to be obvious."

"I'll see you in twenty."

****

Elias followed Bianca to a small secluded park in Camp Springs, Maryland. They parked their cars and walked to a picnic table which was obscured from the parking lot by trees. Upon reaching a park bench they began to kiss passionately. After a few minutes, Bianca pulled away from Elias and looked at him intensely.

"Give it to me doggie-style."

"Out here?"

"Where else?" Bianca began to unbuckle her jeans and loosen her zipper.

"Hold-up. My condoms are in the truck."

"Fuck those things. Give it to me raw dog." Bianca's jeans were down by her ankles revealing red thong underwear.

"Oh yeah!" Elias loosened his belt buckle and let his jeans

fall to his ankles.

"Yes baby, fuck this pussy!" Bianca put her hands on the picnic table and spread her legs after stepping completely out of her jeans.

Elias slid his boxers to his ankles and entered Bianca from the rear. "Sssssssssss."

Bianca moaned. "Yesss, I want all of you."

"Damn girl! This feels good." Elias began to thrust harder and harder.

"Yeah daddy! Take the pussy! Take the pussy!"

Elias thrusted with more force. Faster as the mere minutes seemed like an eternity of pleasure.

"Oh…uh…uh…harder…oh!" Bianca moaned.

"Oh damn…I'm about to come!"

"Yes…yes…go deeper…come in me…come in me."

"Ah shit! Damn!" Elias began to spasm as he released everything he had into Bianca. They both collapsed to the ground breathing very hard. They held each other for a few minutes and then slowly put their jeans back on. They then sat at the picnic table. Elias spoke first.

"What was that all about?"

"What do you mean?"

"You know what I mean. The other times we got together it was always at a motel and always in the missionary position. We definitely used protection. What would your mother say if she saw you out here?"

"My mother's the problem. All my life I had to be perfect for her because as she constantly reminds me she sacrificed so much so I wouldn't struggle like she did.

"Every day growing up around her I had to speak perfectly, walk perfectly and be perfect in damn near anyway. Sometimes I got tired of that shit."

Elias picked up Bianca's hand. "Why don't you tell your mother how you feel? Do you think she'll get mad at you?"

"No she wouldn't. She'll just become more depressed than she already is. She's been that way as long as I can remember. Maybe that's why I put up with her. I saw how hard my mother was working to provide for us so I decided as a child to do whatever it takes to make her happy."

"You decide to become her perfect little girl. Damn but nobody's perfect."

"I had to try anyway."

"Just so you could end up out here having unprotected sex in a public park."

"Please don't judge me. It's not like you resisted." Bianca paused. "Sometimes I need to be…less than perfect."

Elias pulled Bianca to him and hugged her. "I'm not judging you. We all have fucked up parents. It's just unfortunate it has to spill over to us."

"Yes it is." Bianca stood up and took Elias by the hand. "We need to get out of here."

"Yeah I need to get back to the store."

"I have a date to get ready for."

****

Bianca checked her messages on her cell phone and saw that Jeffery called her three times. Bianca sighed and called him back.

Jeffery picked up on the second ring. "Where the hell were you!?! I called you three times."

Bianca stayed calm. "Jeffery, I was over at my mother's. Then I was at a mall. My phone was off for a little while."

"That's all?" Jeffery was relieved. "I was getting worried about you."

"Jeffery, I'm a grown woman. I can take care of myself."

"I know. I just worry about you sometimes."

"You're so sweet. I look forward to seeing you tonight."

"Me too. I'll see you later." Jeffery ended the call and walked to his kitchen to get some water. As he poured the water he wondered who Bianca was spending her time with.

Chapter 10

"Danny it's good to see you. Close the door behind you and have a seat." Jeffery motioned Danny into his office. It was the first time they met face to face since Danny was contracted to create a website for Tyler Enterprises.

"It's good to see you too Mr. Tyler," Danny said as he sat down.

"Danny, I'm only a few years older than you. Call me Jeffery."

"So Jeffery, how do you like the website?"

Jeffery chuckled. "You get right to it don't you?"

"I'm like that sometimes."

"Not a bad way to be. I'll get right down to business. I love the website. It grabbed my attention right away. I talked to the managers at my stores and they've noticed an increase in traffic. Not bad for the new site only being up a couple of weeks. You did a great job."

"Thanks but you are paying me to give my best. If I felt I couldn't produce I wouldn't have signed the contract."

"That's another thing. I need to offer you an apology."

"For what?"

"There was a small part of me that thought you would let me down."

"Really? Well, looking at the previous website I can understand why. No apology is needed though. If you didn't have at least a tiny bit of doubt you wouldn't have made it this far. Any good businessman would be the same way."

"Well said. I don't meet many men like you. Most men are intimidated by me."

"A real man would never be intimidated by another man. You must have been dealing with a lot of punks."

"That's most of my workforce. I personally couldn't work for somebody like me."

"That's interesting."

"What are you doing for lunch?"

"I'm headed over to a spot called *Riley's Place*."

"*Riley's Place*? I haven't heard of it."

"It's a strip club over in Southwest."

Jeffery was surprised. "You're having lunch at a strip club?"

79

"It's stimulation for the taste buds and the groins," Danny grinned.

"You know I've never been to a strip club."

It was Danny's turn to be surprised. "Get out. You've never been to a strip club? It's hard to believe that."

"Believe it."

"You should roll with me. You'll probably enjoy it."

"Maybe…" Jeffery was hesitant. "Why not? Do I need to bring a lot of money?"

"Naw, I sure don't."

****

The music was a little more subdued than usual because of the lunchtime crowd. The men were more sedate in their business attire. Danny was enjoying both his food and the energy he was getting from the women. Jeffery on the other hand, was very uncomfortable with the atmosphere and the attention he was getting from the dancers.

Noticing Jeffery's discomfort Danny suggested that they leave. Jeffery was only too happy to comply. They were silent for few minutes while driving back in Danny's Mustang. Danny decided to break the ice.

"You okay man. You didn't seem too comfortable back there."

"I'm just not comfortable seeing Black women prostituting themselves like that."

"I don't see it as prostitution. It's not like they're having sex. They're just dancing."

"They're dancing in front of men who are giving them money. Sex may not be involved but what they're doing is along the same lines as prostitution."

"To me it's no different than watching a dance troupe."

"We'll just have to agree to disagree."

"I guess. I just know those dancers energize me. They're indirectly responsible for your website."

"I guess they're not that bad then," Jeffery laughed. He looked around at the people on the street. "You ever look at people and feel sorry for them?"

"I do feel sorry for the homeless, especially the homeless kids."

"I feel bad for the homeless and try to do what I can through charity and subsidized housing but they're not the people I'm talking about."

"Who then?"

"I feel sorry for these men and women who have the jobs, homes, and stable lives."

"You feel sorry for ordinary folks?"

"That's just it, they are ordinary. They were ordinary as children growing up in their nice safe homes. They're ordinary as adults and they'll be ordinary when they die. They're not like us. They're ants."

Danny studied the intense look on Jeffery's face as an insight came to him. "You didn't quite have a normal childhood did you?"

"I didn't have much of childhood period. I had to grow up

early. How did you know?"

"Every now and then I look at people the same way you do. Sometimes I think growing up in a normal household might have been cool."

"It sounds like we have more in common than I realized."

"Perhaps."

"Danny, we're not ordinary men. I see it in how you carry yourself. Men like us live by our will and no one else's. We are not followers. We're leaders."

"I feel very ordinary at times."

"If you were truly ordinary you wouldn't have my respect." Jeffery saw that Danny had stopped in front of his office building. "We'll have to get together again. I don't have many people I can relate to."

"Yeah man, we'll talk again. You seem different from the articles in the business journals."

Jeffery grinned as he got out of the car. "There's many facets about me that won't show up in a magazine.

****

Jeffery sat impassively at his desk for nearly fifteen minutes. Then he stood up and walked over to his window. He looked down at the people on the street. In a way they did look like ants.

He thought back to the strip club and his discomfort. Jeffery was glad Danny didn't pry too much. Jeffery didn't want to say that the dancers made him think about his mother.

After his parents' divorce Jeffery stayed with his mother

Sharon. Jeffery noticed a change in his mother almost immediately. His mother began to wear more provocative and alluring clothing. She also began to date a number of men. As Sharon spent more time with different men she began to neglect Jeffery. Even though he was only six at the time Jeffery had to take care of himself. By the time he was eight he was already earning money from lawn work and paper routes. As he grew older Sharon became more like a roommate than a mother. Sometimes they could go days without saying anything to each other. The only exception being when Sharon wanted something from Jeffery.

Sharon would never just ask Jeffery or any other man for something outright. She always used subtle manipulation to get what she wanted. Her weapon of choice was sex appeal. Jeffery seen it work on his father until he got fed up with her games. He saw it work on the different men she brought to the house. Those men disgusted Jeffery in how they groveled to his mother. He made up his mind not to be like those men when he grew up. He vowed never to let a woman control him. Watching his mother he concluded that there was only one way a woman could control a man. He reached this conclusion after one particular incident with his mother.

The phone rang bringing Jeffery out of his thoughts. He was glad for the interruption as he didn't want to relive an unpleasant incident.

Chapter 11

"I'm going to miss you," Yumi said as her head was resting on Danny's chest.

Danny lightly rubbed Yumi's arm. "I'm going to miss you too."

"Stop playing with me Danny. You'll probably be with another woman before the week is out."

"I don't know why you think I have all of these women." Danny took a deep breath. "I meant what I said. I'm going to miss you."

Yumi sat up in the bed. "You're serious aren't you?"

"Yes I am." Danny sat up with Yumi. "Even though our 'relationship' has been mostly in the bedroom I've probably been closer to you than anyone else."

"Are you going to tell me you haven't been close with other women?"

"Not at all though not that many. I just...have always had trouble getting close to women especially Black women."

"Who have you gone out with?"

"A few white women, a couple of Latinas. One very beautiful woman from Japan."

Yumi blushed. "Thank you. You're very beautiful as well."

"Please, I'm ugly."

"Why do you think that?"

Danny looked down at the skin on the back of his hands. "That's what my mother told me."

"I really find that hard to believe. All mothers think their sons are beautiful."

"Mine did. She told me every time she had a chance when I was a little."

Yumi let out a breath of air. "Did your father do anything?"

"You mean my sperm donor as my mother called him. Never met him. I don't even know his name because quite frankly I don't think my mother knew his name."

"Whoa, she didn't know who he was?"

Danny got off the bed and paced the room for a second, took a deep breath and sat back down on the bed. "Remember the other day I told you I met with Jeffery Tyler?"

"Yes."

"We had lunch at *Riley's Place*, that strip club I told you about. We were driving back and somehow we talked about growing up early. I knew he didn't have a childhood because of certain things he said. It made me start thinking about my own childhood or lack thereof.

"From the time I was a baby it was just my mother and me. She worked as, how can I put it delicately…I can't really, she worked as an exotic dancer. That is when she had work. When she got mad at me she would tell me that I was conceived in an alley behind a club. My father, or sperm donor as my mother called him, was an out of town businessman who was very generous with the tips. She said his name was Albert but that could have a fake name. It doesn't matter. Nine months later I came kicking and screaming into the world.

"My mother, Glenda Evans, was estranged from her family so it was just the two of us. My mother didn't have any marketable skills other than dancing so she kept right on doing her thing. My earliest memories are of being held by different dancers as my mother performed. She made good and was able to provide for us and she was even somewhat loving to me. Outside of her dancing she tried to make things as normal as possible for me. As normal as a life could be for a little boy with a mother working in adult entertainment. I learned to take care of myself from the time I could walk. Imagine a little boy who barely reach the stove trying to cook."

Danny chuckled and then continued. "Then one night when I was seven, I believe my mother had a nervous breakdown.

I think that what it was when I look back at things. Whatever it was she lost her mind. She stopped dancing and just laid around the apartment. She would barely leave the place. She would give me money to go to the store. Eventually the money ran out and we were evicted from our place. We had to live on streets for a while, sleeping in parks and sometimes abandoned buildings. It was around this time she started telling me how ugly I was. She said I looked like my father."

Yumi crawled to Danny, put her legs around his waist and held him from the back. "I'm sorry you had to go through that."

Danny cracked a half-smile as Yumi's embrace made him feel good. "Oh it gets 'better.' My mother and I would beg for spare change and sometimes I would go through trash cans and eat what I could find. My mother would use what change she could get and buy alcohol. It proved to be her undoing. She died in her sleep when we were staying in an abandoned apartment building.

"I didn't know what to do. So I left her. In a way I had psychologically left her anyway. I was about nine when she passed. I was on my own for a few months when a man stopped me when I was going through a trash can. He gave me five dollars and I ran off to get something to eat. The five went in like a day. I went back to that same spot looking for that same man. I saw him walking and asked for more money. He, Mr. Irvin, asked about my situation. I told him and he took me to a family services shelter. I was then placed in the foster care system.

"So did everything turn out better for you?" Yumi held Danny tighter.

Danny gently broke Yumi's embrace and stood up. He

walked over to his dresser, tapping it while lost in thought. He then walked by to the bed and sat down next to Yumi. "No it didn't. I was shuttled around to a couple of different homes for a couple of years until I was placed with the Berrys. I was the only foster child under their care. They had a weird relationship in my mind. It was like they were in two separate worlds. Mr. Berry seemed like he did nothing but watch TV and worked. It was like he wanted nothing more out of his life. Mrs. Berry on the other hand was full of life. She was always on the go and she was very caring. A little too caring."

Danny stood up again, took a deep breath and then sat back down. "I lied when I said I never been with a Black woman. I had sex with Mrs. Berry for several years."

"Danny…no. You were so young. That was abuse." Tears began to form in Yumi's eyes.

"Yeah, I came to realize that. You know there is all this talk about little girls getting sexually abused but nothing is said about little boys who are sexually abused. Of course I didn't see it like that. I was just hitting puberty and Mrs. Berry was very attractive and very neglected. It was a young man's fantasy. The only problem was that even though I was physically ready for sex I wasn't emotionally ready. This wasn't a teenage girl I was dealing with. It was a grown woman who was supposed to be a mother figure to me.

"Gradually it made me feel dirty. I remember I told Mrs. Berry I wanted to stop having sex with her. She got mad and started to make the next few months miserable. She wouldn't allow me to have girlfriends, she would get mad and call me ugly. It was just a lot of stuff.

"It got to a point where I couldn't take it anymore. So I packed my things and ran away. I stayed on the streets for about year until I ended up at this group home run by a group of Catholic Nuns. They were very kind to me. It was probably the closest I ever came to believing in God."

"You don't believe in God?" Yumi asked.

"After all I had been through I didn't have a reason to believe. Anyway I stayed at that home until I was eighteen and then I went out into the world."

Yumi reached over and hugged Danny tightly. Her warmth felt good to Danny who returned her hug. "You've been through a lot. You're an extraordinary person."

"Jeffery Tyler seemed to think the same thing." Danny looked Yumi in her eyes. "I'm nothing special. I'm a survivor nothing more, nothing less."

"Many people couldn't have sanely gone through the things that you have. You had to have something to make it as far as you have."

"I made it because of my code."

"Your code?"

"Yeah, despite my hectic life I was an avid reader. I read books on many subjects. While I was at the Catholic house I picked up a couple of books that helped shape my thinking. One was Japanese actually, *The Book of Five Rings* by Musashi Miyamoto and the *Art of War* by Sun Tzu. These books started me on a path. I took from these books and others the best information and incorporated them into my life. I went through a period of cleansing and transformation. I worked on my mind and body. My final act of transformation came when I decided to change my name."

"I was wondering about your name. You said your mother's last name was Evans and you didn't know your father's name," Yumi said.

"My first name wasn't even Danny. It was Matthew. I got the name Danny from that man I told you caught me going through the trash. He really saved my life. "Code," well, I decided to live my life by a certain code. The code of a warrior. A real warrior is not someone who fights all the time. At least not other people. The real battle is within ourselves and against our darker impulses. Every time I say my name or someone calls my name I will be reminded of the path I chose to walk."

"Danny," Yumi stroked Danny's cheek. "You really are extraordinary. I'm very proud of you. You'll always have place in my heart."

"And you in mine."

"A couple of things I want you to consider. Despite what you say I think at some deep level you believe in God."

"What makes you say that? I have no interest in going to church."

"God is bigger than a building. I think you are used to seeing God through American eyes. We see and worship God differently in Japan. We all have our own paths to God. I think without realizing it you created one unique to who you are."

"You sound like a young lady I met a few weeks ago at *Riley's Place*. Her name's Alicia. She's very interesting."

"Is she Black?"

"Yes she is."

Yumi smiled. "I think she may be good for you."

"Why do you say that?"

"Your face lit up when you mentioned her name."

"Oh…I'm sorry. We're just friends."

"For now anyway." Yumi lightly stroked Danny's upper lip. "I love you Danny and I always will but I'm also realistic. I'm going back to Japan next week. My destiny is there. You'll always have a place in my heart and I wish you all the happiness in the world."

"You…love me. I-I don't know what to say."

"You've already said with how you've treated me. Beneath that tough exterior is a very caring person."

"I…I…I'm going to miss you."

"Just think of me every now and then. Reach for your happiness. Maybe I'll come back for your wedding to Alicia."

"Now hold on…" Danny smirked.

"Danny, I'm not some insecure little girl. I see you have some feelings for Alicia. You have to go for it. Besides I'll send you invitation to my wedding. I plan to marry the future prime minister of Japan."

"You have somebody waiting for you."

"No but I won't let that stop me."

Danny and Yumi paused to look at each other and then broke out laughing.

After a minute Danny regained his composure. "I love you too. I can't wait to meet the man who wins your heart."

"I can't wait to meet him myself," Yumi laughed.

"Hey we still have all night," Danny said as he pulled Yumi to him.

Yumi put her arm around Danny's neck. "What do you have in mind?

"Well there's this technique I read about in the *Tao of Sexology*. It's called Sets of Nine."

Chapter 12

Steam was in a different world.

As her body moved sensuously, Steam's mind was at a different level of consciousness, a different reality. A reality where she was the owner of a juice bar. The bar featured organic teas and fruit juices. It was also a place where people could listen to jazz and poetry. This was her dream. In a few more months she would be able to make her dream a reality.

After her set Steam took her tips and went backstage to change her clothes.

She came from the dressing room and walked around thanking the men who tipped her. She stopped when she ran into Elias who was sitting at a table in the back of the club. Elias was nursing a rum and coke drink.

"Hey baby, you okay? I didn't see you back here." Steam leaned down to give Elias a kiss on his cheek.

"I'm just relaxing."

Steam sat down. "I don't know…you're not looking like your usual self. You're usually right up front."

"I just wanted to chill out and think about some things."

"You picked a heck of a place to think."

"Where else would I go? It's always stressful at home. It's not like I can chill out with Bianca."

"Bianca? That's that woman you see occasionally isn't it? The one who's married."

"Nah, she's not married but it's the same difference. Shit she's part of the problem. I have strong feelings for her but she's in a fucked up situation."

Steam laughed. "For a brotha who is about conscious raising you certainly curse and drink a lot."

"You of all people know about the contradictions we all live with," Elias grinned. "Anyway, I get tired of how things are. With my family, with Bianca. You ever wish you could live a different life?"

"As Destiny would say, 'chile please.' When I'm up on stage I have to be in a different world. Many of these men disgust me.

The only pleasure I get from being here is the money and the control I have over these men."

"What else would you do?"

"I haven't told you this but for the last couple of months I've been thinking about opening up a spot where I can serve tea and juices and have poetry readings."

"A coffee house."

"Same principle but no caffeine."

"Are you serious? I think that's great! Have you looked into everything? I can help you with whatever you need."

"Elias you went from melancholy to excited just like that."

"St...Alicia you're a dear friend. I feel closer to you than I do my own family. Anything I can do to help you reach your goals would be an honor for me."

"Thank you Elias. But enough about me. You're the one looking all sad up in here. Anything I can do to help?"

Elias took Steam's hand and squeezed it briefly. "You're helping by caring for me. Just keep being there."

"Okay baby. I have to get ready for my next set. Are you sticking around?" Steam stood up.

"Nah, I have some things I need to take care of," Elias said as he stood up and gave Steam a hug.

"Take care, I love you baby." Steam gave Elias a warm hug.

"I love you too. Don't kick anybody's ass tonight."

Steam smiled as she walked back to the dressing room.

Elias watched her walk away and then headed out of the club to his next destination.

Rom Wills

****

"Who is it?" Bianca yelled as she walked to answer her doorbell.

"It's me," Elias said from the other side of the door.

Bianca sighed as she opened the door. "Elias, this is the second time you've come over unannounced. Why do you continue to disrespect my wishes?"

"Look I'm sorry but I had to see you. Please let me in."

Bianca sighed again. "Come in."

Elias walked in and closed the door behind him. "You're looking good."

"With this on?" Bianca indicated the T-shirt and shorts she had on.

"Especially with what you have on." Elias looked appreciatively at Bianca's shapely body. "You're so beautiful when you're not putting up a front."

Bianca blushed. "I'm not beautiful. I'm too big and too dark."

"Where'd you get that dumb ass idea from?"

"You know I'm not considered beautiful by society's standards. You know a beautiful woman has to be a size 6 or less, white, or light-skinned."

"Fuck society and shit. How the hell did that become the standard? That must have been some shit made up by gay fashion designers. Even white men go for healthy women. Why you think Marilyn Monroe is still popular?"

"She's still white. I don't see anybody who looks like me in

96

the media or magazines."

"Girl come with me to your bedroom."

"My bedroom? Why…"

"Bring your ass on." Elias grabbed Bianca's hand and led her to the bedroom. She was surprised by his forcefulness.

They walked to the full-length mirror and Elias had Bianca stand and look at himself. They looked at the mirror for a minute before Elias spoke. "What do you see?"

"I see a dark-skinned overweight woman."

"That's not what I see."

"What do you see?"

"I see a beautiful Black queen.

"I look at your flawless skin, smooth and perfect, like an obsidian sculpture.

"I look at your beautiful face with its almond eyes, its high cheekbones, its full luscious lips.

"I look at your face in its totality and take in the compassion and sensuality represented in its awesome balance."

Bianca blushed. "Thank you."

Without another word Elias slowly and carefully lifted Bianca's t-shirt over her head and tossed it to the side while admiring her full breasts. He looked her in her eyes as he pulled her shorts and panties to her ankles. He held her hand she stepped out of her clothes and stood her in front of the mirror again as he moved behind her.

"Black queen, Black queen," Elias began. "You are the mother of the universe. You are the center of the universe. Look at your neck and shoulders. Look at how strong and regal they are.

The strength in them…great enough to be enveloped in the embrace of a strong Black man.

"Look at your breasts. Big and full. The milk from those breasts can nurture a nation.

"We move down to your hips as I behold your hour glass figure which arouses all men who behold you.

"Your hips, your hips. Not only do they arouse a man to his full masculinity, but they provide room to carry an infant and to nurture her to adulthood.

"We go down to your shapely legs. They are strong. They are soft. Their power reaches into the Earth itself. Like a mighty oak these legs can withstand all storms and all adversity. I feel their sheer power when they are wrapped around my back.

"Last but certainly not least your butt. Oh my God, your beautiful butt. It's like an upside down heart. It's very sway putting a man into a hypnotic trance causing a man to move heaven and Earth for just a small sample of your precious nectar.

"Black queen, Black queen, you are the symbol of what it means to be a woman. Don't ever look at yourself and feel you don't measure up to anyone's artificial standard.

"Black queen, Black queen, you are the standard. Any real man knows this."

With tears in her eyes Bianca turned to Elias. "Thank you. That was so beautiful."

Elias took Bianca to her bed and gently laid her down. He took in Bianca's beauty as he disrobed. He then moved to the edge of the bed and began kissing and massaging Bianca's feet. First her left and then her right. Bianca began to moan softly as he used his knowledge of reflexology to stimulate her pleasure centers. Using his tongue and hands Elias moved up Bianca's legs eventually reaching her soaking wet womanhood. He teased her with a few flicks of his tongue sending tingles throughout her body.

Elias then flipped Bianca onto her stomach and then started licking her from the small of her back to the nap of her neck, further putting her into a state of sensual intoxication. He flipped her back over, kissing her passionately using his tongue to explore with an intense passion.

He stopped the kiss and worked his way back down kissing her neck, her shoulders, and her breasts. His tongue flicked each breast, teasing them to rock hard perkiness before engulfing the nipples of each breast as her moans grew louder.

Elias finished with Bianca's breasts and moved down her stomach and back to her womanhood where her love juices flowed like a river before a storm. Elias dove in with a fervor causing Bianca to utter a primal grown felt to the very depths of her being.

Elias used his tongue with expert precision and then suddenly stopped, causing Bianca to open her beautiful eyes as the passion between them was communicated on a subliminal level.

Elias moved up to kiss Bianca at the same time entering her slowly causing Bianca to let out a loud moan.

They were in perfect rhythm as they began slowly and then began to increase in speed as their breathing became faster. Elias watched her cues as he knew to increase his intensity.

Bianca began to become more frantic as she wrapped her arms around Elias's neck and squeezed tightly. Her legs raised to wrap themselves around Elias's waist.

The sensual energy began to overwhelm Bianca as she started yelling at Elias to increase his intensity as the sweat began to drip off of them.

The steady rise of energy increased as Bianca could contain herself no longer as she exploded with a series of orgasms causing her entire body to tremble from her quivering vagina to the top of her skull to the soles of her feet. Her orgasms penetrated to the depths of her soul triggering a response by Elias as he trembled and released his essence into Bianca.

For a brief moment Elias and Bianca were united. Two had become one. They breathed with one breath. They thought with one thought. They both fell into a deep sleep where they dreamed the same dream.

Chapter 13

  Bianca was walking down a road when she came to a dead-in street. There were only two houses on this street across from each other. One house was a large mansion with a three car garage, and a big yard. The house looked to be made of wood. Bianca looked and saw Jeffery walking out of the house. He beckoned her to come to him. She started to walk to him but something stopped her. Bianca turned around and looked at the house across the street. It was a smaller house with only a driveway and smaller yard. It was only a rambler but it was all brick with a fireplace. The door to the house opened and

Elias walked out, motioning Bianca to come to him. Bianca glanced back to Jeffery and started walking to Elias. She walked a few feet to the middle of road and then stopped. She glanced between them and was about to take a step when she suddenly heard a phone ringing.

"Ummm, who's calling this early?" Bianca reached for the phone on her night stand. "Hello?"

"Good morning Bianca. Did you sleep well last night?" Jeffery asked.

"Jeffery? What are you doing calling this early on a Saturday morning?" Bianca sat up in her bed.

"It's almost noon. You're usually up early on Saturday mornings."

"Yes I am but I…uh…decided to sleep late this morning. How are you?"

"I'm fine. I'm about to go to the gym. I was wondering what you were doing later today."

"I just have some stuff I need to do around here and for my mother."

"Let do something tonight. Maybe a movie."

"That will be great. Ummm, give me a call this evening. I look forward to seeing you."

"As do I. I'll talk to you soon."

"Yes, we'll speak later," Bianca said as she ended the call and leaned back into the headboard of her bed.

"What are you going to talk about? The intricacies of proper bourgeois behavior?" Elias propped himself up on his elbows.

"Very funny," Bianca smiled. "Last night was great. I've

never experienced anything quite like that. I didn't know that an orgasm could feel like that."

"You haven't had a brother rock your world like that."

"I've had my encounters but not like that"

"None of those bourgie bammas hit it right."

"Not really. Not the 'bourgie bammas' anyway. Sex with them was always...tame. The only satisfaction I got was from the thugs."

Elias sat up. "You used to fuck with thugs?"

"I was not going to be seen in public with them but they handled their business in the bedroom. They even seemed to appreciate me more than the 'good' guys."

"How'd your mother feel about them?"

"She did not know about them. It was all on the down low. That made it exciting. It was my way of rebelling against my mother."

"Did it work?"

Bianca looked at Elias. "It's funny you say it like that. I really wasn't fulfilled."

"Is being with me a form of rebellion?"

"Elias...at first it was. But you're different. I'm starting to have real feelings for you. You're the first man to really treat me like I'm special and not a trophy or a sex toy."

"Jeffery doesn't treat you special."

"I don't know about Jeffery sometimes. He's treats me like a perfect gentleman. I'm neither a sex toy nor a trophy with him. Something though...is missing. I cannot put my finger on it."

"If you're feeling something for me and not sure about

Jeffery you need to be with me. I'm tired of sneaking around."

"I don't know if my mother would approve of you."

"Why shouldn't she?"

"My mother has a color complex. She thinks the only men worth anything were light-skin with wavy hair. They also have to have money."

"Okay so the white man hasn't dipped into my gene pool to the same extent as Jeffery. Does that really make me any less? And no I don't have the same money as Jeffery Tyler. I'm not broke either. I have a degree and a thriving business."

"I know. I really admire that you were able to build a business from scratch. You and Jeffery have that in common. It's just…my mother."

"You need to tell your mother to get a life."

"Elias I can't tell my mother that. She sacrificed a lot for me growing up."

"Maybe she did but you grown now. She ain't still raising you is she?"

"Well no she isn't? Elias you just don't understand."

"Bianca, I understand better than you realize. At least you don't have to live with your mother. Sometimes I wish I could just leave her someplace but I can't…I. Bianca I'm about to tell you something which I've never told anybody. I may look like a punk for saying this but my feelings for you are growing so strong. I want to put my cards out on the table."

Bianca took Elias's hand. "Go ahead. I'm here for you."

Elias took in the compassion which came from Bianca. "I have a problem. I could easily set up my mother and sister in their own apartment or house even but I don't because of my problem."

"What's the issue?"

"I don't like being alone. I have real fear of abandonment. I've been doing some reading and it goes back to my childhood I believe. My mother wasn't the most maternal of women. My father took better care of me than she did. Then he was killed when I was young."

"I'm sorry." Bianca reached out to hug Elias.

"Don't be. It's part of my life mission. I'm not sure what you believe religiously but the beliefs I try to follow state that we are here to evolve and that we all have something we need to work through. What I have to work through is abandonment. It's tough because I feel a void when I'm not around somebody. I think that's why I've always been a hustler because I need to interact with people. I have my mother and sister with me because I don't want to come home to an empty house. I know it may seem like I'm a mama's boy but I'm not."

"Elias I apologize if I made you feel bad for living with your mother. Sometimes we just don't know the whole story. At same time I may not be going through the same thing you're going through but I'm going through my own stuff as well. I don't have the same insight that you do."

"With you, I believe your spiritual mission is to break out of your mental prison. Some people have parents who try to control their every little move. They try to make their children carbon copies of themselves and they try to force their values on their children. On the surface it may seem like the children are complying but in reality they are rebelling underneath. That's exactly what you're doing. Your mother wants you with Jeffery because your mother would get with somebody like Jeffery. You rebel by being with me, somebody your mother wouldn't necessarily like. You can't keep living like that. You have to be true to yourself."

"By being with you openly?"

"The selfish part of me says yes. That's my greatest wish but though it pains me I might not be the one. You have to do what's right for you and only you."

"Elias, I don't know what to say," Bianca said with a tear in her eye.

Elias wiped the tear away from Bianca's eye and then put his arms around her. "You don't have to say anything. Just know that we both need healing."

Bianca and Elias held each other tightly as the intimacy between them reached a new level.

Chapter 14

I...uh...decided to sleep late this morning.

Bianca's words played over and over in Jeffery's mind as he drove to his gym for his workout. His mind drifted to when he was nine years old. His mother Sharon, was in her bedroom with some man she had met two weeks before. Jeffery couldn't recall his name. Sharon was already seeing Mr. Thomas for a few months but fidelity wasn't one of her strong suits. That morning Sharon was in bed with her new lover when the phone rang.

"Hello?" Sharon answered. "Hi Randy...nothing much...I...uh...decided to sleep late this morning."

Jeffery heard everything through the wall. Jeffery hated how his mother manipulated Mr. Thomas because he liked the man.

Jeffery pulled into the parking lot for the health club. He walked past the front desk attendant in a daze. Jeffery walked to the locker room to put up his gym bag and sweat suit. He continued to think about the different men who came to the house. All of them enticed by Sharon's sensual allure, unaware that they were all flies going into the spider's web. No man was safe from her manipulative persona. Not even her own son.

Jeffery usually engaged in weight training when he was at the health club but today he decided on a different workout.

He walked into the room with the boxing equipment and sat down against the wall. He wrapped his hands up and then slipped on sparring gloves. His mind drifted back to when he was twelve years old. His father Eddie took him to a local gym to teach him how to box. Jeffery had been constantly getting into fights with other boys who teased him for being a pretty boy. Jeffery was usually on the losing end. Eddie decided to solve this problem. To Eddie's surprise Jeffery took quickly to boxing. He became so good it was recommended that Jeffery get involved with Golden Gloves. Eddie, didn't want Jeffery to box competitively. He had other plans for his son's future.

Jeffery stood up and walked to the punching bag. He assumed a boxer's stance and looked at the bag as it were an opponent in the ring. Jeffery jabbed at the bag a couple of times with his right and then brought his left up for a combination. He repeated this pattern for a few minutes as he warmed up. As the sweat began to build on his brow he began to think back to the incident that happened when he was fourteen.

He had been hanging out with his father more and more to his mother's chagrin. In his mother's eyes he was becoming more rebellious by not doing things to her liking around the house and talking back more. Sharon didn't know what to do as a mother. She decided to use other methods.

Jeffery was in his room one day sitting on his bed reading a book for his English class. His mother walked in wearing a provocative dress for a date later that night. She asked him how come he hadn't taken out the trash. Jeffery looked at her strangely because he had already taken out the trash. He always did his household chores.

Sharon talked to him differently. Usually she spoke to him in a harsh and slightly hostile tone. That night her voice was soft and seductive.

"I'm proud of how you study all the time," Sharon said.

"Thanks. Are you just noticing how much I study?"

"No, I don't compliment you enough. My you're growing handsome."

"T-Thank you." Jeffery began to feel uncomfortable as his mother put her hand on his thigh and began to rub slowly.

"Yeah Jeff, you're very handsome. I'm surprised that a bunch of little girls aren't calling you every day."

"I don't give them my number. I'm concentrating on school and work. I don't have time for these girls. They're so childish."

"My grown little man, you've always been mature for your age. Maybe you need an older woman to stoke your fires."

"Stoke my fires?" Jeffery saw a strange look in his mother's eyes.

"Yeah, stoke your fires. At fourteen, I know you've starting to feel different."

"I do have more energy."

"Yeah but you're putting it into school and work. There are other uses for that energy." Sharon leaned in and kissed Jeffery lightly on his lips. She studied his bewildered look and then kissed him again as Jeffery responded briefly before pushing her off of him onto the floor.

"What the hell are you doing!?!" Jeffery yelled.

"I…I'm sorry." Sharon looked up from the floor. "I don't know what came over me."

"You whore!!! I'm your son!!! What the hell is wrong with you!?!"

"I don't know." Sharon looked down at the floor.

"I'm your son." Jeffery walked out of the room and left the house. He moved in with his father the next day. He never told his father the reason he wanted to leave Sharon's house.

Jeffery began to release his full fury into the punching bag. He remembered the hurt and pain he felt after the incident. The pain that was coming up now.

Harder and harder he punched.

He thought about when he lived with his father and working in his father's business, Tyler Enterprises, which bought old properties, renovated them and sold them to new homeowners. Jeffery worked hard with his father learning all aspects of business until his father's death.

For the most part living and working with his father was okay. The only time it was a problem was when his father asked him about his love life. Jeffery just didn't seem as interested in girls. Eddie didn't know what to make of his son. He didn't want to think Jeffery was gay but still there were questions.

Jeffery began to grunt as he tore into the punching bag.

Jeffery started dating some of the girls who were showing interest, more for appearances than anything else. He never tried to have sex with them because they reminded him of his mother. Jeffery had determined that the woman he wanted would be the opposite of his mother.

He thought he had found that woman in Bianca but after talking with her this morning he wasn't so sure.

Jeffery let out a primal yell as he unloaded a powerful left hand into the punching and then collapsed to the floor breathing very hard.

Chapter 15

"Hi Alicia, I hope this isn't a bad time," Danny said into the phone.

"Not at all. I just finished doing some yoga," Alicia answered.

"How was work?"

"Same ol'. This one dork gave me close to one hundred dollars."

Danny laughed. "For that much money you must have gave him a little something extra."

"Some people just appreciate my art."

"I never heard it called an art before."

"Hey baby, anything I do is an art."

Danny and Alicia shared a laugh before Danny spoke again.

"How would you like to see a movie tonight? *The Best Mack.*"

"I would love to except I have my brother with me."

"You told me about your brother. I don't want to mess that up. What are you two doing?"

"We usually just walk around a mall and go to a movie."

"Well I haven't met your brother yet…you mind if I hang with y'all? My treat."

"Danny, you don't have to do that."

"I don't mind. It's not like I'm going to a strip club tonight."

Alicia laughed. "You have a good sense of humor for somebody who's looking serious all the time."

"I'm full of surprises."

"I'm sure you are. I accept your offer. I have to pick up my brother in a few. We can meet at the mall tonight."

"I'll pick you up like a gentleman is supposed to do. I'll call you about five to get directions to your place. I look forward to seeing you"

"Me too. I'll talk to you later Danny. Peace."

"Later." Danny hung up the phone smiling as he reached for the remote to see what was on TV.

****

"I...I...I win!" Solomon smiled as he looked up from the arcade game.

"Good going man," Danny said. "You're good at killing mutants."

"Okay."

"Boy I keep telling you to say thank you." Alicia smiled. She was pleased that Danny and Solomon were getting along very well.

"Ah leave him alone. You're such a mom," Danny said.

"I had to be with Solomon," Alicia said solemnly.

Danny decided to change the subject. "Y'all want something to eat?"

"Yeah!" Solomon yelled.

The three of them walked to the food court in the mall. Danny bought chicken wings for himself, a cheeseburger and fries for Solomon, and a veggie burger for Alicia. They sat down at a table and started talking about the movie they had just seen.

"I...I...It wasn't that good. I...I...I didn't laugh that much. They didn't act that good," Solomon said.

Alicia laughed. "Now tell us how you really feel. Don't hold back."

"Okay."

"That wasn't one of my man's better movies. He needs to stick to the Black Buppie movies. He needs to leave the wannabe playa movies to real comedians," Danny said.

Alicia frowned. "You guys. The movie wasn't that bad. We gotta support our Black films."

"I...I...It was bad," Solomon said.

"You usually like films like that one."

"Not that one Lish."

Danny interrupted. "I understand what you're saying about supporting Black films but we need to be at least putting out quality films. The movie just lacked a whole lot."

Alicia sighed. "You guys. You gotta see the good in everything."

"That's a beautiful thing. You really have a good heart," Danny said.

Alicia blushed. "Thank you. You're so sweet."

"G...G...Get a room," Solomon said.

"Boy!" Alicia yelled.

Danny grinned.

****

"You were great with Solly," Alicia said. She and Danny were back at her apartment after they dropped Solomon off at his group home.

Danny nodded his head. He was amazed at the number of books Alicia had lying around. "He's a great kid. There's a lot of love between you two."

"I pretty much raised him. I'll be glad when I have enough money to buy a house and really support us.

"I thought you were getting paid dancing."

"I do but I'm saving most of that for a future business. I don't plan to dance forever."

"What type of business do you want to get into?"

"I want to open a juice bar."

"A juice bar? Wow. You know that's funny."

"What?"

"When I first saw you I was focused on how beautiful and sexy you were. There is so much more to you. I mean on one hand you're the sexy exotic dancer Steam and on the other hand you're the very sweet, very thoughtful, very intelligent, even more beautiful Alicia."

"Thank you."

"You ever think about the contradictions."

"The contradictions?"

Danny shifted in his seat. "Yeah. I mean I see a contradiction in you. Myself. Everybody really. One part of us we show society...our masks. Then there is another part that very few people get to see...our true selves."

"I know what you are talking about," Alicia said. "You're talking about duality. Duality is at the core of everything in existence. Day and night, Light and dark, hot and cold, male and female. Duality is everywhere, especially within us."

"That's what I'm saying."

"That's my existence every day. On one hand there's Steam. Sexy. Bold. Then there's Alicia. Shy. Bookish. Two opposites and yet they exist in one being."

"Are you in a battle within yourself?"

"You know, it funny but I'm not. Steam and Alicia are comfortable with each other. One they complement each other. They are not two conflicting personas but different aspects of the same persona. It's like a sports car that looks nice and sleek. It's good to look at one hand but on the other hand it can blow away the other cars on the highway. Looking good and being powerful are two aspects of the same car.

"Steam is my sensual aspect. I can use her to make money. Alicia allows me to express my intellectual side. I don't have to suppress who I am. I think that's what gets people into trouble. We all have a sensual side and a spiritual side. The problem is that people think one must be expressed at the expense of the other."

Danny chimed in. "I see it all the time. People are either out there with their sensuality or they suppress their sensuality with their intellect. People believe they can only be one or the other. Why not both?"

"Exactly! It's dangerous to suppress our nature. What we do have to do is make sure it doesn't get out of control but the two sides can live side by side no matter what people think. It's just a matter of coming to the center of two points. Did I ever tell you why I call myself 'Steam' when I'm dancing?"

"No you haven't."

"As you know I read a lot of metaphysical books. One book dealt with personality types. As a dancer I express a water personality which is yin, sensual, and in the body. As Alicia though, I express a fire personality which is more yang and in the head. What happens when you mix fire and water?"

"Well water puts out fire…hmmmm, it creates steam."

"That's one way of looking at it. Fire can also warm up a pot of water. In other words though fire and water can be antagonistic by combining them in a complementary fashion they can work together."

"Damn that's deep. You're a fascinating individual."

"Thank you. You very fascinating to me."

"I am?" Danny was surprised. "I'm just an ordinary Joe."

"Whatever you are, you're not ordinary. I study people. There's something more to you. A mystery, a complexity. Who are you really? Before you became 'Danny Code.'"

Danny looked at Alicia. "Why do you say it like that?"

"I just know there's more to you. I know that 'Danny Code' is self-created."

"What makes you say that?"

"The way you walk. The way you talk. Everything about you. Most people are shaped by outside forces be it religion, social norms, or the media. You, Danny, are above those things. You are a powerful man. Society doesn't create powerful men. It makes men weak. I can't stand weak men."

Danny thought he saw a slight change in Alicia's expression as she continued talking. "You live by your own code. I wouldn't be surprised if Code isn't your real name. You probably gave it to yourself."

Danny was startled. "That's incredible. How did you know?"

"I see with my third eye. One day you'll tell me your story."

"What makes you think I won't tell you now?"

"You're not ready. Just like I'm not ready to tell you about me."

Alicia got up and walked over to the chair Danny was sitting in and held her hand out.

Danny took it and pulled Alicia to his lap and kissed her lightly on her lips and then held her.

After a few minutes Alicia looked into Danny's eyes. "I look forward to getting to know you."

"Me too," Danny said as he touched his forehead to Alicia's forehead. They looked into each other's eyes.

Nothing was said.

Everything was understood.

Chapter 16

Jeffery was at peace as he stood out on the large patio of his Ft. Washington, Maryland, home that overlooked the Potomac River. His home was in a secluded location away from the public. His hideaway where he could take off the mask of perfection he felt he needed to wear in the world. Even Bianca hadn't been to his home. Perhaps he needed to open up to her more. Maybe in time.

I...uh...decided to sleep late this morning.

Jeffery winced. Those words have been playing in his head

ever since Bianca said them. Did she have another man? Could he blame her? Was she really different from any other woman?

Jeffery turned and walked back into his bedroom. Most people would be impressed at the size of his home and that he had a patio connected to his upstairs bedroom. If he allowed people to even come his home.

He walked to his full length mirror. People would think he looked nice in his tailored dark indigo Armani suit and expensive leather slip-ons. Jeffery chuckled when he thought about the times people would ask him if he was a model. Sometimes he thought about giving away his clothes, selling his home, business, and just work as a handyman for the rest of his life. He really enjoyed working with his father fixing up houses.

Jeffery's thoughts were interrupted when he heard the distinctive ring tone of his cell phone. When he picked the phone off of the dresser he sighed, breathed in deeply, and pushed the icon to speak. "Hello mother."

"My you sound so formal," Jeffery's mother Sharon said on the other end.

Jeffery was a little irritated. "What do you want?"

"Is that any way to talk to your mother? I raised you better than that."

"What do you want?" Jeffery breathed in deeply to keep from losing his composure. Sharon Tyler was the type of woman to go for the jugular if a man showed any weakness in her presence.

"I can't call just to talk to my very handsome son?"

Jeffery sighed again. "Mother you never call unless you want something."

"Maybe I called just to talk." Sharon giggled as she spoke. Jeffery immediately thought she was up to something.

"I really don't have time to talk now. I'm about to go out now."

"You have a date with that healthy young woman. What's her name, Bianca?"

"Yes mother."

"She's very beautiful with her smooth dark skin. You two would make beautiful babies. I know you hitting it right." Sharon's tone was sarcastic.

"What we do is our business." Jeffery's voice cracked slightly.

Sharon laughed. "You haven't had sex with her yet. You probably never will even if you marry her. I hope you're cool with letting her sleep with other men."

"That's uncalled for. What we do is our business," Jeffery said as his heart started to beat faster. He couldn't let his mother know she was messing with his head.

"Um hmm," Sharon smirked as she sensed the opening. "The great and fine Jeffery Tyler. Still a virgin. I'm surprised a woman hasn't raped you. You fine just like your daddy. I wish I knew what was wrong with you because I know you ain't gay."

"You know what mother, I have to go see Bianca. This is the last time we'll have this conversation," Jeffery said with steel in his voice.

"My fine, fine son. You know ain't no man telling me what to do. We will have this conversation again if I so choose." Sharon then laughed. "Maybe it's a good thing you are scared of pussy.   Some ratchet would empty your bank account."

Jeffery steadied his breathing.   "Are you through mother?"

"For now baby.   I would tell you to get that big girl to suck your dick but we know that ain't happening.   We'll talk later. Bye." Sharon ended the call.

Jeffery looked at his phone thinking, "typical."   He needed to regain his composure because as usual Sharon Tyler knew how to rattle her son.

****

"That program I'm sponsoring is really helping those autistic children."   Jeffery and Bianca were having a chicken dinner at *Marco's,* an exclusive restaurant in Georgetown.   The dinner anyplace else would have cost $4.95.

"That's good Jeffery.   You really do a lot of good with your money."   Bianca was wearing a light beige evening dress.   Bianca though had been distant all night.

"Yeah I have to give back.   People need help and I'm blessed to be able to provide it." Jeffery studied Bianca.   She seemed like she was just going through the motions.   "Are you enjoying the dinner?"

"The food is good."   Bianca really wasn't moved by the food.   Her mind was elsewhere.   "You have any big charity projects coming up?"

Jeffery used a napkin to wipe the side of his mouth. "Nothing really.   I get a lot of requests but unfortunately I can't support everybody.   I have to feel something for any project."

"So you felt something for the autistic kids?"

"Yes I did. The program focuses on recognizing the gifts of these children. Many of them are very talented but in different ways. We just have to teach them differently."

Bianca looked at Jeffery. One thing she admired about him was that he was sincere in trying to help people. Times like this she wished their relationship was different. It was then she heard her phone's ringtone, Led Zeppelin's *Kashmir.* "Hold on Jeffery, I got a text." Bianca saw it was from Elias. He wanted to come see her later that night. Bianca smiled slightly as she texted back, "Yes."

Jeffery noticed Bianca's slight smile. "Who was that?

"Just my mother," Bianca said calmly.

Jeffery masked his skepticism. "How is she?"

"Still crazy," Bianca smiled.

"It's getting late. Let me pay for this expensive dinner and get you home."

****

Bianca sat on her living room couch with nothing on but a silver silk robe. She was already wet from thinking about Elias. Jeffery had dropped her off earlier in the evening and true to form gave her a kiss on the cheek. Bianca wasted no time in getting out of her clothes, grabbing the silk robe, and sitting on her couch in anticipation after texting Elias to come over.

As she sat on the couch she felt mild contractions and started to shake a little. Oh yeah she was ready. She bolted up after hearing her door bell. She opened the door to see Elias in a T-shirt and jeans. "Damn you look good Elias."

Elias smiled. "You look go…"

Immediately, Bianca pulled Elias in the door, closed and locked it and started exploring his mouth like she hadn't seen him in years. As they were kissing Elias took the robe off and grabbed Bianca's ass like he was holding on for dear life.

Bianca unbuckled Elias's pants and yanked them down along with his boxers exposing a rock hard manhood. Bianca immediately got to her knees and took Elias into her mouth as if she had been waiting years for this moment.

Elias and Bianca was so into the moment they didn't think about the lights and that the drapes were open enough for someone outside to see their shadows.

Someone like Jeffery Tyler.

Chapter 17

Jeffery walked through the mall oblivious to everything and everyone around him. He ignored the professional women giving him appreciative looks. He did not notice the teenage girls giggling when they saw him. He certainly paid no attention to the jealous men. Jeffery could have cared less. He didn't dress for attention as he wore a plain black athletic T shirt and sweat pants. He wasn't at the mall to be seen.

He was on a mission.

His thoughts went back to his dinner with Bianca a few days

ago. She claimed to have received a text from her mother which caused her to smile. There was one problem.

Bianca's mother didn't have a cell phone.

Jeffery remembered a conversation with Bianca where she complained that her mother refused to get a cell phone. Her mother didn't feel like she needed one and plus she believed the conspiracy theories about cell phones causing brain damage.

Jeffery knew that she was lying.

I...uh...decided to sleep late this morning.

When Jeffery dropped Bianca off he drove to a spot where he could see her building and waited. He didn't have long to wait. A Ford Expedition pulled up in the parking lot and a tall Black man got out and went into Bianca's building. At that point Jeffery got out so he could take a closer look. As he suspected the man went to Bianca's condo and without regard to who may have seen them, they engaged in some very indecent acts.

Jeffery felt his anger rise as he watched HIS woman give this man a blow job. He kept his composure and walked over to the license plates and took a picture with his smartphone. He had some contacts in the local police departments and was able to match a name to the man violating HIS woman.

Elias Robbins.

Turns out Elias had a pretty profitable bookstore. Jeffery found the store's website and was actually impressed with Elias and the business he had built up. Elias was a man who was above the ants like himself. Under different circumstances they may have become business associates. Even friends.

Jeffery wasn't going to allow Elias to take his honor. One

thing that Jeffery learned from his father was that at the end of the day honor was all a man had. It was more important than even money. Obviously this Elias had no honor.

Jeffery arrived at *Robbins Books*. He would look Elias in the eye and determine what type of man he was.

There were a few people in the store. Elias was walking around talking to different people when he looked up and saw him. Jeffery Tyler was in his store.

They held each other's gaze like the legendary gunfighters of the old west. They communicated in a nano-second in a way that only men understood. Elias knew that Jeffery knew about him and Bianca. Jeffery knew Elias was the man violating HIS woman. Jeffery grew up boxing. Despite his money, despite his low key fame, despite his looks, he was ready to knuckle up and deal with this disrespect like the old school men.

He was ready to throw hands.

Elias recognized the look in his eye. He hadn't seen it in a long time but recognized it nonetheless. Elias wasn't a punk though. Underneath his fun-loving exterior was a man who had been in more than a few street fights. Elias had also trained a few times with some brothas who were into little known martial art systems such as Neo-Ngolo and 52 Blocks.

Elias wasn't going to be punked in his own store.

He was ready to throw hands.

Jeffery and Elias stepped to each other. No words were needed. The universe it seemed had other plans.

"What's up fellas? Imagine seeing you both here."

Jeffery and Elias turned to see Danny Code walking towards

them. Danny sensed the tension between them. Danny's instincts told him that they were about to fight. Probably over a woman.

Elias smiled, "Hey, hey Danny. Came in to get your usual fix?" Elias gave Danny the one-armed hug brothas give each other.

"Yeah, I came in to see what you got." Danny turned to Jeffery. "Small world. I thought you lived on the other side of the county?"

Jeffery paused for a second before speaking. "I like to check out *little* bookstores."

Both Danny and Elias caught the emphasis on the word "little."

"Well you know sometimes *little* can do the job that something supposedly bigger can't do." Elias studied Jeffery's reaction. No emotion. The dig didn't affect him. This pretty nigga had some street in him. Elias thought that under different circumstances he and Jeffery could have been business associates. Even friends.

Danny felt he needed to diffuse whatever the hell was going on. "Y'all two know each other."

They both answered no.

Danny held his hands out to both of them. "Elias Robbins, Jeffery Tyler."

Elias held his hand out to Jeffery. "*The* Jeffery Tyler? An honor to have you in my little store."

"I see my reputation precedes me." Jeffery shook Elias's hand with a firm grip. Elias had an equally firm grip. Jeffery despite everything was impressed. Too bad they had to meet under these circumstances. "I like your store." Jeffery was sincere.

"Thank you." Elias relaxed a little but still stayed alert.

Danny still sensing some tension decided to jump in. "Yeah Jeffery, I love coming here. My man, Elias, got books on everything." Danny looked at Elias. "You get that new book on street fighting in the Black community?"

Elias looked at Danny thinking about the irony of his question. "Nah, not yet. I got plenty of other martial arts books though."

"Street fighting?" Jeffery had a questioning look on his face.

"Yeah," Danny responded. "The book gets into how back in the day men settled things with their fists and not with guns like these punks do nowadays."

Jeffery smiled. "I remembered those days. A man had to fight straight up."

"None of the grabbing shit or rassling like the old timers would say," Elias added.

Jeffery went on. "A man had to box. It wasn't about winning or losing but standing up for yourself."

"Often the man who kicked your ass would have your back the next week," Danny said. "Heck the two would become lifelong friends. There was a code back then. Something we as Black men have lost."

"There's still pockets of it," Jeffery said. "They are becoming few and far between. What we have now is a disgrace."

Elias shook his head. "Tell me about it. I look at these young brothas out here with their pants hanging off their ass thinking they men."

Danny shook his head as well. "You can tell them that sagging started in prisons as a way for men to show that they were open for sex. It's like these young boys want someone to go inside of them."

"Young boys? Heck you got grown men walking around with their pants off their ass," Jeffery said. "Man my father would have planted his size twelves up my ass if I even thought about wearing my pants like that."

"Your father?" Elias chuckled. "My father would have whipped my butt for even thinking about doing something like that." Elias without thinking reached his fist to Jeffery for a pound.

Jeffery hesitated for a split second and then pounded Elias's fist. Damn, Elias was a man like himself.

Elias thought that Jeffery wasn't as bad as he thought. He felt bad for a second. Then an image of Bianca with her smooth chocolate booty in the air erased any feelings of guilt.

Danny jumped in the conversation. "You two are lucky you had your fathers in your lives. I didn't really have that."

Jeffery looked at Danny. "You didn't? That's surprising. You carry yourself with honor. Like a warrior. I was thinking your father may have been in the service."

"No I got the way I am through hard work," Danny said.

"Whatever you did it works," Elias said.

Jeffery nodded his head in agreement.

Danny continued, "It was tough going but I think I've done something with my life. It's too bad many Black boys out here are not making it."

"They need their fathers in their lives," Jeffery said. "It

makes a big difference.   Many of these single mothers are not doing the job they think they are."

Elias thought he saw a familiar look in Jeffery's eyes for a second.   The same look he would often see while looking in the mirror.   "Men, especially Black men, just need to stand up.   We need that warrior spirit we once had.   Now more than ever."

"Like Jeffery said, there's pockets of us keeping the spirit alive.   Men like ourselves have to be examples and live as warriors," Danny said with a profound look on his face.

"Yes.   Like warriors."   Jeffery nodded his head.   He came to the store to fight Elias.   Was this the way to go?   He needed to think.   "Elias it was good meeting you.   Maybe I will check out your store again."   He extended his hand to Elias.

Elias shook Jeffery's hand.   "Good meeting you too."   The feeling of guilt crept back in.   Jeffery wasn't that bad a person. Was his actions with Bianca honorable?   He needed to think.

Without another word Jeffery left the store.

Danny took in everything.   There were some things going on that they were not saying.   He wondered about the woman who nearly caused these two men to come to blows.

Chapter 18

Danny drove through the streets of the working class neighborhood in Northeast, DC in a calm state. Coltrane and Miles were playing jazz music that shifted his consciousness to prepare him for his date with Alicia. He was at peace. Or as Alicia said from that book she told him about, *Metu Neter,* a state of Amen Hetep.

Danny chuckled about all the books Alicia told him about. For a stripper she was into all that new agey stuff. Then again, Danny was into at least one thing that would be considered new agey.   Maybe he would get to share that with Alicia tonight.

Danny smiled as he thought about Alicia.   He didn't think that he would ever develop feelings for a Black woman.   Only Danny Code could fall for a stripper, book nerd, Plain Jane, a little quirky, a little shy, all wrapped into a sista who could probably break his spine if he didn't come correct.

Now that's love right there.

Danny pulled up behind Alicia's old 1994 Toyota Nissan which according to her ran just fine.   Hey it got her from point A to point B and that's all Alicia cared about.   Even though she could afford a newer car she was saving her money for her bar.

Damn, a beautiful sista who was down to earth and good with money.

Danny thought he needed to marry her.   He was surprised Alicia didn't have any men trying to lock her down.

Danny parked and stepped out of his blue Mustang.   He was usually modest but he knew he was looking good.   Got him a fresh haircut that afternoon.   He had on a white cotton fitted shirt open at the collar revealing a simple but elegant silver chain.   The shirt flowed well with his gunmetal gray slacks and gray Italian slip-ons.

A few young women walking by Alicia's small apartment building gave Danny some appreciative looks.   He smiled back at them acknowledging their own beauty.

Something must have come over him, Danny thought.   He usually ignored women giving him attention.   It seemed like since he met Alicia his perception about many things was changing.

He walked in through the door to the building, up the stairs to Alicia's apartment, and knocked on the door. Alicia responded. "Come in, it's open."

Danny walked in and was still amazed at the number of books she had lying around.

"Are you ready to go?"

Danny turned around and nearly stopped breathing. His manhood came alive with a jolt. He heard something in his head say, "How you doing?" Was his dick talking to him?

"You okay Danny?" Alicia was clearly amused as she looked at Danny's crotch. Didn't really faze her. She was used to a man reacting to her in that way.

"I need to sit down for a second." Danny sat down on the couch and breathed deeply and looked up at Alicia. She was wearing a wine colored short spandex dress that clinged to every curve of her lovely body showing off her perfectly round booty and shapely legs. Her hair looked like she just came from the salon and her face was perfect with subtle but perfectly applied makeup. She was Steam and yet Alicia. It was like she was at the perfect balance point between her two personas. "Why didn't you warn a brotha? Damn baby you're a lethal weapon."

Alicia turned around slowly for Danny. "So you like what you see?" She stopped and gave him a full view of her backside and then turned to face him.

"Girl how you gonna do me like that? As it is we won't be able to leave for ten minutes," Danny said, still trying to regain his composure. He figured his hard-on would relax enough in ten minutes to drive.

Alicia sat down next to Danny giggling like a kid. "I'm

sorry baby." She pulled Danny to her and kissed his forehead. "This is so funny."

"No it isn't." Danny was still breathing hard.

Alicia laughed. "Yes it is. I got the serious, never smiling action hero Danny Code to lose his cool. I'm always going to remember this moment." She rubbed his back. "Don't worry, this will be our special moment."

Danny started laughing so hard he fell back on the couch. It felt good to be this comfortable around a woman. Though he had been with quite a few he was never this comfortable, not even with Yumi. "Ah man. You ready to go?"

"Yes I am."

Danny stood up and held out his hand to help Alicia up. "Let's get out of here."

A voice in his head said, "Bump that, pull out the sofa bed!" Danny's manhood really was talking to him.

****

Danny and Alicia arrived at *Erotique* and got in right away. Danny wasn't used to waiting in lines anyway. He and Alicia walked right to the front and the bouncer gave Danny the customary fist pound and let him in. As they were walking by, the bouncer caught Danny's eye and mouthed the words, "That you?" Danny nodded and the bouncer grinned and they gave each other another fist pound.

Danny and Alicia wasted no time as they went straight to

the dance floor. Danny admired how sensuous Alicia was when she danced. Unlike at the strip club where as Steam she would be in her own world her eyes were fixed on Danny.

Alicia was continually surprised by Danny. First she saw him lose his cool at her place earlier and now he pulled one more thing out of his bag of tricks.

Danny could dance his ass off.

Most men would do some type of moving not necessarily on the beat. Usually a two-step going side to side. Watching Danny he had become one with the music. The Alicia side of the persona was impressed. The Steam side of the persona thought Danny could make a lot of money as a male stripper.

Danny was the most interesting man she had ever met.

After 45 minutes straight dancing the DJ put on a reggae jam. Danny and Alicia began to move as one as if a palpable energy was going back and forth between them. Alicia went into a mild trance as she turned and bent over slightly. Danny took the invitation and he put his strong hands around her waist and locked his fingers together. Alicia started grinding on Danny's fully engorged manhood in a rhythmic circular motion. Her mouth parted slightly as the tip of her tongue touched the roof of her mouth. She grinded deeper and deeper on Danny as his manhood responded with a steady pulse that synced with the bass in the slow sensuous reggae song that spoke of a love that spanned centuries.

Alicia began to lose gradual awareness of her surroundings as the multitude of people in the club became just her and Danny.

Alicia felt the strength in Danny's hands as they enveloped her in a protective embrace. He was her shield against the world.

Her knight who would protect her against all who would harm her. The yang to her yin. As he held her she rubbed his strong arms feeling the power in them. The power of the warrior to protect her. The power of the hunter to provide for her. The power of the eagle to see the path ahead. The power of the healer to make her whole.

The house of the man in all its glory.

Alicia felt Danny's power in not just his hands but in his manhood as the steady pulse of energy ran throughout Alicia building up a pressure she could no longer contain.

"Oh, oh, oh," Alicia said softly as her vagina began contracting sending waves of pleasure throughout her body.

Danny recognizing that Alicia was having orgasms released his hold on her and turned her around to embrace her tightly. Her pelvis found his pulsing manhood again and surrendered to the moment. Alicia felt energy coming from Danny's hands as they rubbed her back. Danny piercing gaze looked into the depths of Alicia's soul and found a beautiful spirit that needed the embrace of a strong man. A man who could spin a cocoon for her and allow Alicia to grow into a beautiful butterfly.

"Oh, oh, oh." Alicia felt Danny's energy penetrate her on many levels. Damn who is this man? Who is Danny Code?

Alicia didn't know it could be like this. Dare she tell him her secret? Yes. She didn't know why but she felt she could tell Danny anything and he would not judge her. He would accept her. He would hold her and protect her. He would make love to her. He would make her feel truly beautiful.

"Ohhhhh." Alicia rested her head on Danny's shoulder.

His strong broad shoulder. Alicia let the energy of the final orgasm stay with her for a seeming eternity. "How did you...do that?"

Danny looked at Alicia with his pretty almond eyes. "I'm into some new agey things myself." Danny smiled. "You ready to get out of here?"

"Yeah let's go."

****

Danny and Alicia start kissing passionately as soon as they walked through the apartment door. Alicia felt the same energy from Danny she felt at the club.   As much as she hated to, Alicia forced herself to break their embrace. She walked over to the couch and sat down.

Danny walled over and sat down next to her. "What's wrong?"

Alicia looked at Danny with tears in her eyes. "Before we go further I have to truly open myself to you. I need to tell you my story."

Chapter 19

Alicia looked into Danny's eyes as they sat together on the couch. They had so much warmth and compassion in them at that moment. She still felt Danny's power as he held her hand firmly.

"Take your time Alicia. I'm here for you. With me you can be free," Danny said with a confidence that Alicia had never heard from a man before.

Alicia breathed in and out slowly with her eyes closed, then she slowly opened them. "My story. I grew up outside of Baltimore in Edgewood, Md. It was me and my mother, Lauren, at first. She didn't deal with my biological father after I was born. The feeling I got was that they didn't have that serious of a relationship. It was tough going for my mother at first. She did the best she could but she was also working all the time. I remember staying with my grandmother a lot before she passed away. When I was about five years old my mother met this…man named Vernon. Eventually he moved in with us. *I ain' like em though.*"

Danny detected a change in Alicia's tone and speech intonation. She sounded like a little girl.

Alicia kept talking, still sounding like a little girl. "*I ain' like Mistah Vernon. He made me feel fraid when he look at me. There was sump'in in his eyes. I scared. I was fraid to tell mommy. Mistah Vernon would rub my bun-bun when mommy ain' around. He rub my chest sayin they'll be nice. He told me to be quiet or I would get in trouble.*"

"My God." Danny pulled Alicia to him and held her tighter, gently stroked her face.

"*I was so fraid. I didn't want trouble with mommy. He show me his ding-a-ling. He made me touch it. He wanted to stick it in my private place but mommy had told me not to let a boy touch there til I was older. So I ran. He ain' try no more but he kept rubbing me. He did it for years. I would read books to get away. I pretended I was a strong woman who could fight him. He kept touching me anyway. He gave me money to keep quiet. It got worse while mommy was carrying Solly. Then he tried to stick it in again…*" Alicia started breathing very hard and was shaking. Danny held on tighter but then Alicia suddenly pulled away from him and stood up. Her whole demeanor changed as she walked around the room. Even her body language was different. Alicia was no longer in the room.

"Alicia started the story. I'm here to finish it," Steam said. "That nigga Vernon pushed things too fucking far. That night he tried to stick his little ass dick in me. I kicked him in his teeny tiny balls and ran out the room. I went to the kitchen and got a knife and was ready to cut that shit. He came in the kitchen trying to calm me down. That's when my mother came home tired from work, pregnant with Solly. She looked at her ten year girl with a knife in her hands and that nigga Vernon in a wife beater and boxers. She asked what was going on. Vernon said I was crazy. He had the nerve to say that I disobeyed him when he told me to clean up my room.

"My mother looked at Vernon and then looked at me. She walked over to me calmly and took the knife out of my hands. I'll never forget that moment. I saw so much love in her eyes. I looked over at Vernon. He had a smug look on his face like he had won the lottery. My mother looked at Vernon and then looked back at me and smiled. She rubbed my hair gently. She then turned to Vernon.

"Nigga I will cut your god damn dick off!"

"She lunged at Vernon slashing wildly. The smug look on his face turned to fear as moved to dodge the knife thrusts. He made it to the door and ran out into the night. My mother looked at him running away. She locked the door behind him and turned to me and said, 'Baby I am so sorry. Tell me everything while we clean.' I asked her what we were cleaning. She said we were going to throw Vernon's stuff out."

Steam rolled her neck around as if she was relieving some stress. She sat down next to Danny. Danny wanted to hold her again but Steam at that moment didn't seem to want to be touched.

Steam nodded her head. "You know that's the last time I saw Vernon."

Danny looked at her. "Do you know what happened to him?"

Steam smiled. "I'm not exactly sure. I know my mother made a phone call that night and that she whispered the whole time. I know a month later they found Vernon's body in a park on the Eastern Shore. Apparently someone had castrated him."

The normally cool Danny Code gulped.

"My mother and I got closer after that. After Solly was born it was just the three of us. Well maybe four of us. Alicia was the one who took care of him while mother worked and hit the books. I helped bring money in."

Danny looked at her. "How?"

"Oh I didn't sleep with anybody. I did pop out a nice booty when I hit twelve. I mean it had been nice already if I do say so myself. It just got better. I got a lot of attention from the boys at school. It amazed me that teenaged boys would give a few dollars just to feel up on a girl."

"That's all they did?"

Steam looked at Danny and smiled. She stroked his strong jaw lightly with her finger. Then suddenly her smile faded. Danny felt her energy shift. Alicia was back with him.

"Danny you see many things with those pretty eyes of yours but they can't see everything." Alicia gently grabbed Danny's hand.

143

"Danny, nothing happened because I'm a virgin." Alicia started giggling.

"Why are you giggling?" Danny was stunned. Nothing about Alicia/Steam's energy said virgin.

Alicia giggled even more. "Twice in one day. I take the great action hero Danny Code by surprise once again."

Danny laughed. "You read a lot of comic books when you were young didn't you?"

"Watched all the superhero shows too."

Danny and Alicia both laughed and then put their arms around each other. They embraced quietly for several minutes in silence until Alicia gently pulled away.

"Believe it or not I'm a virgin. I mean I, or rather Steam would let boys feel us up. She even gave a couple of hand jobs but she...rather I...we never let any boy penetrate us. Funny we always felt we needed to wait for someone special." Alicia gently rubbed Danny's eye brows.

Danny looked at Alicia intently. His eyes communicating that she was safe with him.

Alicia gasped from looking into Danny's eyes. "I was supposed to go to college but my mother passed away from a brain tumor. I had to work and take care of Solly. I also had to go through some bull to retain custody of him. I let Steam deal with the men at child services. Needless to say we were able to keep custody.

"I wasn't able to keep on top of things working retail and at fast food places. That's when Steam got the first job at a low level strip club. I've always had the ambition of owning a business though. While Steam was dancing and bringing in money I was hitting the books on success, metaphysics, juicing, and taking yoga. Steam though got a black belt in American Karate and trained in Muay Thai and boxing with this real thorough brotha who was like a father figure to us, Baba Kofi."

"Baba Kofi?" Danny masked his surprise at hearing the familiar name.

"Yeah. He was an old friend of my mother. He would come around every now and then. They weren't romantic or anything."

Danny didn't believe in God the way other people did but he did believe there was no such thing as coincidences. The "Baba Kofi" he met a long time ago was a hitman trained in several fighting disciplines with a preference for killing with blades. The Baba Kofi he remembered had an intense hatred for child molesters. He would have had no problem killing someone like Vernon. Danny made a mental note to talk with Alicia later about him. There were some things he wasn't ready to reveal about himself. Presently, he needed to confirm an observation he had made about Alicia. "So how did you deal with the split personality issue or what they call it now, Dissociative Identity Disorder?"

Alicia smiled. "Beauty and brains. You're a keeper Danny Code." Alicia breathed in and out rhythmically. Alicia closed her eyes.

Steam opened them again. "Who said it was a disorder?" Steam closed her eyes.

Alicia opened her eyes. "We were separate at one time."

145

Alicia closed her eyes.

Steam opened them. "That is no longer the case." Steam closed her eyes.

Alicia spoke, "We are two sides of the same coin. I am the spiritual."

Steam spoke, "I am the carnal."

"We are heaven and Earth combined as one. We don't suppress who we are. We are one. We…I am one." Alicia/Steam stood up and walked around the room.

Danny saw the two energies combined as they walked around. A thought hit him as they moved about. "Was there a twin who died in childbirth?"

"Yes." Alicia/Steam looked at Danny. How did he know? Who is he? What's behind those eyes?

"What do I call you?" Danny was curious as to the answer.

"Alicia will be fine except when we are working. Then you can call me Steam. Does this surprise you?"

Danny scrunched his face a bit. "Naw."

They both started laughing as Alicia sat back down.

Alicia looked at Danny. "I want you to be the first." Alicia started rubbing on Danny's chest. Danny grabbed her hand to move it away.

"Don't you want this?" Alicia looked into Danny's eyes for some clue as to why he moved her hand away.

"Yes. More than anything. But not now. Not here. Your first time will be special. I will set everything up. After all I have to make love to two women."

Alicia laughed. "You never cease to amaze me Danny

146

Code."

Danny and Alicia held each other the rest of the night.

Chapter 20

Bianca stared at the clothes hanging in her spacious walk-in closet and sighed. She was standing in her bathrobe, frowning with disappointment. Yes she had stylish professional clothes and expensive shoes but everything was so...drab. The clothes were perfect for working a corporate job and her evening dresses were very elegant but she wanted something...funkier.

Bianca smiled to herself. Ever since she started spending more time with Elias she had been feeling bolder. Being with him made her realize how trapped she had been for years. She always had to put on a perfect front. In school she always had to speak with perfect diction and have her hair done just right. Her clothes could never have a wrinkle in them, conservative though they were. Even when her mother would take her to church she couldn't get into the spirit like everybody else. She always had to be mommy's perfect little girl. She always had to sit up straight, and cross her legs just right. Even when her mother allowed her to go to a couple of school dances with a few of the friends she had she could never really cut loose and enjoy herself. She had to be mindful of every move, every gesture, every glance.

Even when mommy wasn't around Bianca had to be mommy's perfect little girl.

But there were times she wasn't so perfect.

There was those times as a high school freshman she would let a few older boys feel her up at different hidden places around the school. She knew they would never tell because they all had girlfriends. Bianca made a point of only dealing with boys with girlfriends because if they opened their mouths she could threaten to tell their girlfriends. After all Bianca Jennings could never be caught letting boys feel her up.

She was mommy's perfect little girl.

Even in college and afterwards she only dealt with men who were either involved or the thug brothas she knew wouldn't catch feelings. She could truly be free with them.

Oh she tried to be in normal relationships but for some reason the men could never truly turn her on. The few times she would have sex with a "regular" guy it would be quick and unfulfilling. She could only come close to orgasm when it was another woman's man.

When she became involved with Jeffery Tyler a part of her was relieved that Jeffery never pressed her about sex. Maybe he was one of those Christian men who believed in waiting until marriage for sex. Then again Jeffery never really talked about church. Whatever the case the relationship was perfect for her. Jeffery was the very image of an ideal man. He was handsome with a light complexion and rich. He was almost perfect except for a thuggish side that would pop out every now and then. There was a part of her that wanted to see that side.

The most important thing about Jeffery was that her mother approved of him.

Jeffery Tyler was the perfect man for mommy's little girl.

Except that Bianca wasn't a little girl.

She was a grown woman who was tired of living out her mother's dreams.

Maybe that was the appeal of Elias Robbins. Her mother definitely would not approve of him. First of all he wasn't light-skinned and her mother would have definitely had problems with her perfect little girl being with a man who looked more East African than African-American. Her mother would have had a problem with a man who owned a bookstore. Where's the money in that? Especially with everything being sold online. How would it look if Bianca married such a man? She was supposed to be with a professional and not a shop owner. Her mother would have a stroke if she found out that Elias came from the streets.

Bianca smiled. Maybe that's why she liked Elias.

Bianca's smile turned to a frown as she looked around her

closet. She definitely needed to upgrade her wardrobe. She knew just the place to go.

****

"You'll definitely enjoy this book. It gets deep into the history of the ancient African high cultures," Elias said as he put the thick book and the receipt into a bag and handed them to an older brotha with graying locs. "We should have some new books coming this coming Thursday Bro. Jabari."

"Asante Sana Bro. Elias. Stay strong," Bro. Jabari responded.

Elias stooped down to look at some paper work behind the counter when he heard a familiar voice.

"Working hard I see."

Elias smiled as he stood up. Bianca was standing in front of him wearing a plain red t-shirt and some jeans. Though she dressed in a plain manner there was something different about her. Elias shared his observation. "You look very relaxed. Like a burden just fell off your shoulders." Elias walked around the counter to hug and kiss Bianca lightly. Bianca surprised him when she gave him a deep tongue kiss.

Elias stepped back after the kiss. "Wooo. What got into you? Whatever it is you need to get into it some more."

Bianca laughed. Elias always felt that Bianca didn't smile and laugh enough. When she did laugh it always genuine and heartfelt. Her smile could light up a room.

Elias chuckled. "So what did get into you?"

151

Bianca got closer to Elias and rubbed his waist. "You did."

"Oh man. I need to get into you some more." Elias rubbed Bianca's back.

"Oh you will," Bianca teased. It felt good to be openly playful like this with a man. Bianca was never big on public displays of affection.

"So what brings you down here? I know I'm fine and sexy and all. I know you can't keep your hands off of me but we could do that in more...private settings." Elias liked Bianca's new assertiveness.

"Well I didn't come down here just to see you." Bianca stuck her tongue out at Elias and smiled.

Elias smirked, "Ah girl you know you want all this."

Bianca looked Elias up and down. "All that and more." She stroked Elias's face lightly. "Seriously I came to the mall to shop for new clothes."

Elias raised an eyebrow and looked at Bianca with skepticism. "Ain't you the one who said you would, and I quote, 'never shop at this ghetto ass mall?' What changed your mind?"

"I said ghetto ass?"

"Yeah you did. That's how I knew you were serious."

Bianca gave Elias a sheepish grin. "Welllll. You know I might have been a little harsh."

"A little." Elias held up his thumb and forefinger. "You said you didn't want to shop at the same stores as Shaniqua and them."

"Now Elias you know I didn't say 'and them.'"

"Okay maybe I added that. Straight up though. What

152

changed your mind about shopping here?"

Bianca sighed. "I need a change. I need some more stylish clothes."

"You dress pretty fly to me. Just saying."

"Thank you but they are professional clothes. I need something that shows the joy I'm starting to feel. The joy I'm starting to feel because of you."

"Thank you." Elias had to choke back a tear. That was the most special thing anyone had ever said to him. "I'm honored."

"Well I'll let you get back to your work. Wish me luck."

"Luck?"

"I'm used to buying clothes for work and nights on the town. Not clothes just to express myself."

"Can I come with you?"

"Don't you have to work?"

"One of my workers is about to come back from her break. Plus I'm kinda cool with the boss."

Bianca smiled her pretty smile. "I'd be honored to have you come along."

"Thank you my lady." Elias did a half bow. "Let's hit up that lingerie store around the corner first."

Bianca gave Elias a stern look and then started laughing.

Chapter 21

"Maybe I shouldn't have come to this mall to shop."
Bianca took a bite into her pepperoni pizza slice.

Elias took a sip of his orange soda. "There were some cute
outfits."

"Yes, cute for someone size zero. I swear they must not
think size 14 women want to look good." Bianca used her napkin to
wipe the corner of her mouth.

"Even when you're slumming as you call it you're still so
proper," Elias chuckled as he watched Bianca dab at her mouth.

"I may be slumming but I'm still going to have good manners." Bianca made a face crossing her eyes and sticking her tongue out.

Elias laughed as he leaned back in his seat. "You know I'm really feeling this new relaxed you."

"I feel like I can be free around you," Bianca said as she took another bite of her pizza while looking at the cheese pizza on Elias's plate. "You didn't want any meat on it?"

"I'm on the journey to becoming a vegan." Elias thought briefly about his alcohol consumption. He needed to slow down there as well. "Plus I haven't eaten pepperoni since this Muslim brotha told me it was made from swine."

"Now Elias you know those Muslim brothers will sneak a pork chop and a white woman in when they can."

"Ah shit you fucking me up. Clowning people and what-not."

"I'm just letting go. I am sick and tired of wearing a mask for people. I feel like I've spent my entire life pleasing other people. My mother. Jeffery. Whatever the hell he really wants. People on my job. I am ready to do me."

Elias sat up. "Speaking of Jeffery, that bamma came by the store a couple weeks ago. I don't feel like it was random. I have a feeling he may know about us."

Bianca just shrugged.

"You're not concerned?" Elias raised his left eye brow.

"It's not like we have a real relationship. We have been "together" for well over a year and we have barely kissed and we sure haven't had sex. I don't feel like he's gay. To be honest with you I wonder if he's with me to show he's down with Black folks. You know how some of those light skin Black men can be. It can be anything. I only put up with it because he was what my mother would want."

"You're mother needs to live her own life. Jeffery though when he came to the store seemed like he was ready to fight. I would have obliged his octoroon looking ass but this brotha named Danny Code came in and somehow calmed both of us down."

"Danny Code? Sounds like a secret agent. You and Jeffery were about to fight? Did he say something?"

"Not really but it's one of those things that men, especially those from the streets really understand. No words were needed. Let me tell you something about men. We have a way of communicating with each other that goes over the head of a woman listening to that conversation. At least that's how it used to be. I'm not sure about these young boys nowadays.

"An elder sister author named Leslie who grew up around a gang of brothers and male cousins broke it down the best cause her peoples broke it down for her. She said that in the presence of women men will have three conversations at once. The one women will hear. The one men will mean and the slick shit that only the men will get. There's a lot about men even the smartest women will never get. Yeah me and Jeffery had that conversation. A female listening wouldn't have picked up on anything. Luckily the ish got diffused by Danny but I know it's not over."

"That explains why Jeffery has been so distant lately. Ah well." Bianca finished her pizza and took a sip of her grape drink. She then dabbed the side of her mouth with her napkin.

"You're certainly taking this calmly."

Bianca shrugged her shoulders again. "It's not like it was a real relationship. I'm tired of hiding just to be with you."

Elias leaned back into his seat. "So what about your mother? Won't she be disappointed?"

"I can't be my mother's perfect little girl forever. I have to live for myself."

Elias sat up again. "Mothers are a trip. Yours is trying to live through you. Mine refuses to grow up. I really wish Debbie would grow up."

"You call your mother by her first name?"

"She never encouraged me to call her anything else. She certainly didn't act like a mother."

"Well we're a perfect match. Two people with mommy issues."

"A match made in heaven. Maybe that's why we click." Elias sighed. "Enough about our jacked up mamas. How come you didn't like any of the clothes we looked at?"

"Weren't you paying attention? None of them were my size."

"Well really I was looking at your body. Damn you got a nice ass."

Bianca smiled despite herself. "Is that all you see when you're with me?"

"You do have a pretty face and big breastesses."

"Elias I don't know what to do with you." Bianca shook her head.

Elias gave Bianca a seductive look. "I can think of some

Rom Wills

things."

"Oh Elias. Wait until later sexy." Bianca gave Elias an under look that made his manhood come alive. "Right now I'm disappointed I couldn't find something in my size."

"What about the stuff at those stores for women with more...curvy figures?"

"You must be kidding. I would look better wrapping a table cloth around me. I wish there were more stylish and funkier clothes for women of my size."

Elias stroked his chin thoughtfully. "You know you could open your own store selling those types of clothes. I'm sure there are some clothing designers who have what curvy sistas want to wear. Open up a store and get those designers in there. Problem solved."

Bianca looked at Elias for a few seconds. "You may have something there."

"Really, I wasn't that serious."

"Don't give me that Elias. I help run a bank where I deal with business owners every day. You, you my beautiful man, you're not just a business owner but you're a hustler."

"What you know about hustlers?"

"I may have been with a hustler or two on the low back in the day."

Elias raised his left eyebrow again.

Bianca continued, "You're a hustler. A true to the game hustler sees the business opportunity in everything. You think I could be a business owner?"

"I don't see why not. You have to want it though. Money

158

isn't steady at first and you might have to give up some things. The reward makes everything worth it. Ask me how I know."

"Maybe we can talk about it tomorrow morning."

"Why not tonight? I thought you wanted me to come over."

"I do. We won't be talking much. I have to back that thing up."

Elias was really feeling the change in Bianca. "Oh damn."

Chapter 22

So it had come to this, Jeffery thought as he parked his car in front of the modest size house off of Connecticut Ave in upper Northwest DC. At least she kept the yard and house immaculate. Jeffery looked at the late model Mercedes sitting in the driveway and thought that despite her faults she at least had style. He couldn't believe he was here. He rang the doorbell and was surprised when a young chocolate-complexioned man who could not have been no more than twenty answered the door wearing a Washington football jersey and some skinny jeans. Really?

The young man tried to look and sound tough. "Who're you and why you here?"

Sigh. "I'm here to see my mother." Jeffery thought this had to be a new low even for her.

The young man turned and yelled towards the steps leading upstairs. "Ms. LaCroix! Some dude say he here to see his mama! That you!" The young man turned back to Jeffery and looked him up and down.

Jeffery surprised himself by staying generally calm as he walked into the house. Even though the young man was muscular something about him looked like he had a glass jaw. Jeffery thought about the nice navy blue Armani suit he had on and didn't want to break a sweat for this punk.

"Oh my God! What do we have here? This is quite a surprise." Jeffery's mother, Sharon, walked down the stairs to the foyer wearing a red low cut halter top and a short black mini skirt with fishnet stockings and four inch pumps. She walked down the steps slowly and sensually. The young man visibly showed his approval.

Damn she's over the top, Jeffery thought. Why couldn't he have a reasonably normal mother like it seemed everyone else had?

Jeffery tensed up as Sharon walked up and gave him an uncomfortably sensual hug and lingering kiss on his cheek.

The young man seemed to be jealous. "Yo who dis Ms. LaCroix?"

Sharon turned to the young man and flashed a perfect straight and white smile. "This is my son Jeffery. Jeffery this is my...friend, Junior."

161

Junior? Jeffery left the young man hanging as he extended his hand. "Mother we need to talk."

Sharon stepped back and looked at Jeffery for a second and then turned to Junior. "Why don't you be a dear and give my son and I some time alone. Maybe an hour or so." Sharon walked over to a stand by the door and seductively bent slightly to get her car keys. "Take the Mercedes out for a drive."

"Ah man thanks Ms. LaCroix." Junior enthusiastically grabbed the car keys and gave a lingering look to Sharon as he slowly took in her beauty from her light eyes, and her brown slightly wavy shoulder length hair to her voluptuous breasts and shapely legs. Junior found it hard to believe that she was in her late fifties. She certainly had the energy of someone much younger.

Sharon watched Junior and smiled to herself slightly. She then turned to Jeffery and saw a look of disgust on his face. She smiled even more as she walked into her living room from the foyer and sat down on the plush black leather couch and slowly crossed her legs. "So what brings my handsome son out to see his mother? Did you feel I needed some company?"

"I don't think you'll ever lack for company." Jeffery unbuttoned his suit jacket and sat down on an easy chair that matched the leather couch. "Ms. LaCroix? You don't let him call you by your first name? You even went back to your maiden name."

"I am old enough to be his mother. Maybe even his grandmother the way these fast young women are these days. There's still a place for old fashioned respect. As far as LaCroix...I've been feeling an urge to get back to our Creole roots.

162

You know, I haven't made good old fashion gumbo since you were little."

Jeffery chuckled despite himself. "You did make some good gumbo. Dad and I could never get enough."

Sharon giggled. "Those were good times. I'm quite sure though you didn't come over here to reminisce about old times."

Jeffery stood up and started pacing the room. He then sat back down. Though he tried to maintain his composure it was obvious he was upset over something. Sharon smiled slightly and then spoke. "You know Jeffery despite many mistakes on my part I still love and care for you. Tell your mother what's wrong. I'm far from perfect and I haven't sat in a confession booth in years for fear of making the priests blush but your mother has seen...and done a lot. Tell me what bothers you. Is it Bianca?"

Jeffery looked Sharon squarely in her eyes. "How did you know?"

Sharon titled her head slightly giving Jeffery a very seductive look. "Jeffery my beautiful son. Women know. Only dumb women can't read a man. She break my boy's heart?"

"I found out she's been cheating on me. A few weeks ago I saw her give another man a blow job."

"Interesting. Where were they?" Sharon sat back on the couch and got comfortable. She liked scandalous stories.

"They were at her condo. The shades were drawn but I could still see the shadows."

"So the big businessman Jeffery Tyler has reduced himself to being a stalker." Sharon laughed and shook her head.

"This isn't funny mother."

"Oh yes it is. What did you expect?" Sharon got real serious. "Bianca is a beautiful and shapely young lady. Men would do anything to get with someone like her. How long did you think it would be before someone with some "swag" as the young people say and a big enough dick would get to her? A woman like that isn't going to wait for marriage. I knew this would happen. So what are you going to do about it?"

"What do you mean?" Jeffery knew exactly what his mother meant.

"Yes she was going to cheat but she was sloppy about it. Plus that man disrespected you by taking having your woman take him in her mouth. Didn't you learn anything from me?"

"I did confront him," Jeffery said with his head down.

Sharon uncrossed her legs and leaned forward. "Aw sookie, sookie now." Sharon always got turned on by stories of men fighting.

"I ran his plates and went to his place of business. We were about come to blows but it was diffused by a mutual friend of ours. I hate to say it but there were things I admired about the man. Under different circumstances we could be have been friends."

"Fuck friendship! What about your honor!?!" Sharon surprised herself by raising her voice. She breathed in and out slowly before speaking again. "I know your daddy taught you how to fight with your hands but honor...honor. You got that from your LaCroix blood. That man you think you could be buddy buddy with took your honor. You're not some Joe Schmoe working a regular job who has to put up with any bullshit. You're

Jeffery Tyler. I had serious issues with your father's people but one thing I respected about them was that they were fighters. And the men in my family. My people. The LaCroix men would have killed a man for violating their women. A couple actually have. That's where you come from!" Sharon pounded her fists on her thighs to emphasize her argument.

Jeffery looked at his mother differently. He had to admit she was right.

Sharon recognized the look in Jeffery's eyes. "Jeffery Tyler. Jeffery LaCroix. You have the blood of honorable men running through your veins. It's time to regain you honor."

A look came over Jeffery as he stood up. "Yes I have to regain my honor. I have to do what I have to do."

As Jeffery because lost in his thoughts he didn't notice the smile that crept across the face of Sharon LaCroix.

Chapter 23

       Elias woke from a beer induced nap when he heard a car pull into the driveway. The engine was a little louder than usual which meant that it was an older car belonging to one of Debbie's "friends." Elias pushed himself up from the easy chair in his basement. The big screen TV was showing some corny movie. Couldn't have been too interesting if he fell asleep Elias thought. Elias wished he could have spent that Friday night with Bianca but she had to take her mother to some church function. Even though Elias wasn't Christian he would have loved it if his mother went to some type of church if for nothing but to meet a better class of men.

Elias smiled to himself as he walked up the steps. Knowing his mother she would probably be the sidepiece to the reverend. Still it would be a step up for her.

Elias walked through the basement door and towards the foyer. Debbie hadn't come in yet which meant one thing. Time to break up the party.

Elias opened the front door quickly and through the glass storm door he saw what looked to be an older man with a big belly, tongue kissing his mother. Elias thought about the phrase from his youth, "slobbering her down." Well this fat bamma was doing that as well as having his hand up Debbie's way too short gold dress. Elias actually thought she had relative style in an old ratchet way. It was time to end this madness. Elias cleared his throat loudly.

Debbie and the man stopped kissing and looked up. Debbie noted that the look Elias had on his face was the same one her grandfather would have when she brought boys to the house. "Elias you're up."

"A loud car woke me up." Elias looked at the man with Debbie. "Peace bruh."

"What's up young?" The man regarded Elias with a brief look of curiosity and then smiled showing several silver teeth.

Debbie was stunned for a second. Elias was usually hostile towards the men she brought home. "Delroy this is my son Elias.

Elias, Delroy."

Delroy extended his hand which Elias surprised himself by shaking. "Your mother has told me a lot about you."

"She has?" Elias gave his mother a look.

Delroy smiled even more. "She told me about your bookstore. It's great to see young bruhs doing something for themselves. I wish I had something going."

"You don't have a job?" Elias thought, here we go again.

"As they say I'm between jobs." Delroy shrugged his shoulders.

Of course, Elias thought. "I guess you do what you gotta do."

Delroy nodded his head several times. "Got that right young."

"Good meeting you man." Elias turned to his mother. "De...mom. I'll be inside."

Elias walked back to the basement door and walked down the steps. He went back to easy chair and sat down. He grabbed the remote to mute the sound on the TV. He really didn't feel like listening to the corny dialogue coming from the television. A few minutes later Debbie came down the steps. She had a more serious demeanor than she usually did. She sat down on the plush couch that was next to the easy chair.

"So what was that about?" Debbie's tone was more straight forward than usual.

"What was what about?" Elias barely looked at her as his eyes were transfixed on the corny but increasingly interesting movie about the goings on at a mental hospital.

"Don't act stupid baby boy. That the first time you have ever been friendly to one of my friends."

"It is? Well there's a first time for everything."

"I just want to know why?"

"You know mom…sometimes a man gets tired of beating his head against a wall. You're a grown ass woman. As long as none your friends try to harm you or take shit out of my house you can do whatever with them."

Debbie sucked her teeth. "Whatever. Sounding like my grandfather." Debbie thought about her grandfather, Big Jimmy. He was the only father figure she had after her father left her mother.

"From what you told me about him I take that as an honor." The movie really was becoming interesting. He wanted to turn up the sound.

"So why you tripping" Why were you so nice to him?"

Elias decided he was going to have to catch the movie another time. Something told him things were about to get deep. He turned off the TV and sat up in the easy chair to face his mother better. "Like I said I'm tired of beating my head against the wall. I thought that's what you wanted mom?"

"That's another thing what's with this 'mom' stuff. My name is Debbie. I never taught you to call me mom."

Elias breathed in and out slowly. Elias silently thanked the Ancestors for the yoga and meditation teachers. "Now why didn't you teach me to call you mom?"

"I'm was too young to be someone's mom anyway. Calling me Debbie was just fine."

169

"No mom it wasn't. You told me that the only reason you got married was that Pops got you pregnant and that you were still a teenager marrying a man ten years older than you. Yeah I know Big Jimmy didn't believe in any unwed mothers. Dang though Debbie you were still a mother regardless."

"I was still a baby. I don't care what nobody says. A baby that fell for a fine nigga with a big dick. I still wasn't ready to be nobody's mama. Even when your daddy got killed and I got with another fine nigga with a big dick and had your sister I wasn't ready. I missed out on so much."

"You should have kept your god damned legs closed then," Elias said with venom in his voice.

"What!?!"

"Did I stutter?" Elias was scary calm.

Debbie became a little nervous. "W…why would you say something like that?"

"You know what my problem is…mom. My problem is that while you were trying to be a little girl I had to grow up. Quickly. I stopped being a little boy when Pops was killed. Yeah you think it's cool to act like a child forever don't you?"

"It's not like that."

"Isn't it? You've always had some man to take care of you. Big Jimmy, Pops, the Government, whatever hustlers and lowlifes that came through, me."

Debbie looked at Elias strangely. "You."

"Yes me. Why do you think I started hustling? Those welfare checks and food stamps weren't going to get us through the month. Who do you think made sure the bills got paid while you

were partying all the time? I'll give you props for at least having a
checking account. One of the few responsible things you did. You
ever wonder how the bills got paid since you seemed to forget
about your responsibilities. I forged your signature more times
than I care to remember."

"Why would you forge my signature?"

"Having the electric cut off when there was money in the
bank is some bullshit. I wasn't going to sit in the dark because my
mother was too flaky to pay a bill on time or was more concerned
about what to wear to impress some low rent bammas at a cabaret."

"You really thought that about me?"

"I didn't have to think. It was right there. At a time when
I should have been worried about getting picked on the playground
for basketball I had to make sure the bills were paid and food was
on the table. Even when you went and had Lanisha I probably
changed more of her diapers than you did."

"Now you're exaggerating."

"I wish I was. You know mom or Debbie or whatever the
hell you want to be called. I'm tired. Just tired. I'm tired of
dealing with your shit. You're a grown woman. If you want to
chase or be chased by old bammas that's on you. Do you. I've
come to accept that you will never be a mother to me. I'm at peace
with that. I'm not going to let my image of what you should be
hold me hostage. At the same time I'm not going to feed into your
issues. You're my mother regardless. Though you've behaved like
my child I'm going to remind you every chance I get that you are a
mother, my mother. Whether or not you act like it is up to you.
I'm not going to get upset with what you do or don't do. For the

first time in my life I'm at peace."

        Elias stood up and walked upstairs without looking back.

        Debbie sat back on the couch, lost in thought.

Chapter 24

Alicia couldn't ever remember being this excited. The day was finally here. Alicia woke up early that Saturday morning to pack some personal items. Danny said they would spend Saturday night at a secluded home in Powhatan, Virginia. Danny took care of everything.

As Alicia packed she wondered what Danny was up to. It had been two weeks since they went dancing and she had not seen him. Sure they talked and texted each other but for some reason Danny wanted them to stay apart. Whatever was on Danny's mind, it worked. The anticipation alone was getting her hot.

Alicia imagined running her hands through Danny's Caesar haircut and seeing him looking rough and hot.

She imagined the feeling the same energy she felt while dancing.

She was ready to let go.

Alicia finished packing and sat down for a second. She thought about when she was dancing at the club the other night. She had just finished her set when Thunder approached her.

"So you have a big night coming?" Thunder tended to be direct.

Steam acted a little coy. "What are you talking about?"

"Look at you blushing. That fine chocolate brotha 'bout to give you some of that good-good ain't he?"

"Girl I don't know what you are talking about," Steam said as she changed clothes for her next set.

Thunder looked directly at Steam with a smirk. "Baby girl stop playing. You about to become a real woman. You 'bout to get bust wide open."

Steam looked at Thunder for a second and then grabbed her arm and pulled her to the side and spoke in a low tone. "How did you know?"

"Girl who you talking too? Please." Thunder used her right hand to flick her blond weave. "I always knew you were a virgin. It's how you move. Yeah these clowns and tricks in here go crazy over you and make it rain. It's not for your dancing. It's 'cause you so pretty. Really too pretty for this place." Thunder lowered her head with a sad look on her face.

Steam used her hand to raise Thunder's head. "I don't look any prettier than anybody here especially you." Steam always admired Thunder's smooth brown complexion. Thunder though looked like she had weathered some storms in life.

Thunder smiled, "Thanks baby girl. I know he must be special. You give off a glow whenever he's here. What's his name?"

"Danny. Danny Code."

"Sounds like something from a movie."

Steam laughed at Thunder's comment.

Alicia's thoughts were interrupted when her cellphone gave off its distinctive ringtone.

The text was from Danny. It said: **Come outside now.**

Alicia looked out her window and saw a stretch limo and three muscular brothas. She thought Danny must have been in the car.

Alicia looked at her outfit which was very casual. It was jeans and a long sleeve T-shirt. Danny told her she didn't need to bring or even wear anything special. Alicia grabbed her bag and had to remain calm so she didn't run down the steps. She thought about shifting to her Steam persona but Steam would have just run outside.

Alicia walked out of her building and to the limo. She got a closer look at the three muscular brothas. One was standing at the front of the car on the sidewalk. He looked to be about 6'6" and looked like a bigger meaner version of Danny. The big brotha had on a black suit, black neck tie and crisp white shirt. He looked like a Muslim brotha except he had locs that went down to the middle of his back. He also had an Adinkra symbol from West Africa tattooed on his neck. From the book she read it was *Denkyem*, the crocodile. The symbol of adaptability.

Alicia glanced at the brotha standing at the end of the limo.

He was shorter by a few inches and mocha complexioned. He was leaner but still well-muscled. He was wearing a black suit and had locs as well though his only went down to his shoulders. Alicia saw a tattoo on his neck as well. It was *Akofena,* the sword of war. It was a symbol of courage, valor, and heroism.

These were Danny's friends? Their energy was different from the average man on the street but at the same time similar to Danny's energy. Alicia's thoughts were interrupted by the third man who was standing by the car door.

"Good morning Ms. Green. I will be your driver to the destination. My name is Bro. Osei." The brotha had locs and was dressed the same as the others. The only difference was that he was very light-complexioned and may have been able to pass for white except for his long and thick locs.

Alicia instinctively looked at his neck and saw an Adinkra symbol. His symbol was *Nkyinkyim,* twisting. It meant initiative, dynamism, and versatility.

Suddenly Alicia's cellphone buzzed. It was a text from Danny: **I trust these men with my life. You are safe with them.**

Alicia smiled and then got into the car expecting to see Danny but it was empty except for a mini fridge which she opened to find several fruit juices, and water.

"If you need anything Ms. Green, press that button on the door panel and I will get you anything you need," Bro. Osei said.

Alicia got comfortable in her seat. "Thank you."

Bro. Osei closed the door and walked around to the driver's side of the car. There was a partition that separated the passenger area from the driver. The car looked to be top of the line.

Alicia noticed that the other two men got into smaller cars that were in front of and behind the limo. She looked at the cars and noticed that there was at least one other man in each car.

Alicia felt like a head of state going a major meeting. She felt special that Danny had did all of this on her behalf.

****

Alicia had napped during the trip. Bro. Osei at her request played soft jazz and somehow the smell of sandalwood permeated the car. Though very relaxed and half asleep Alicia paid attention to her surroundings the whole time. They had pulled off the highway and drove on a back road for a few miles until they turned into a property. All that was visible was the dirt path that cut through some trees. They drove until the cars emerged at a clearing that had a large house. The car stopped and Bro. Osei got out and opened the passenger side door for Alicia. She saw the men who had greeted her initially standing around as if on guard. She looked towards the house and saw an older Black woman with long gray locs, wearing an African style dress. The woman, though older, was in great shape and had a beautiful chocolate complexion and perfect smile. Alicia wondered if she had an Adinkra tattoo. Alicia smiled when she saw it because it was one she liked personally because it reminded her of her mother. It was *Akoko Nan,* leg of a hen. It meant the hen treads on her chicks but does not kill them. It was a symbol of tough love.

Seeing the men and women reminded her of Baba Kofi.

Rom Wills

Baba Kofi had been the one to give her the book on Adinkra symbols. Alicia thought about a conversation she overheard between her mother and Baba Kofi. They were talking about a group of which he was a member. The group was somewhat underground in the sense that no one seemed to know about them. Baba Kofi was trying to convince her mother to join. What did he call it? The Sankofa Collective.

"Welcome Ms. Green," the older woman said. "My name is Mama Akosua. We're here to get you ready for your evening with...Danny."

"You can call me Alicia." Alicia noted that Mama Akosua seemed ready to call Danny something else. She didn't think his real name was Danny anyway.

Alicia walked into the house and saw there were several young women in the living room. They all had neck tattoos, natural hair ranging from locs, twists, and short afros. They all wore African clothing.

They immediately went to work on her. Alicia was treated to a full day of pampering. It was like being at a full service day spa. From the looks of things it was just a regular house except for several pieces of African art and sculptures. The young women working on her were professional. She received a facial, a manicure, and pedicure. She really enjoyed the full body massage. Someone even did her hair. On top of that they fed her some great vegan food.

Around sundown that evening, the last of the women had left except for Mama Akosua. She looked at Alicia and smiled. "He is a good man. He will heal you. And he is here in this house

178

now.   I will leave you two alone."

"Thank you for everything Mama," Alicia said.

Mama Akosua smiled and embraced Alicia. She started praying in a language that Alicia didn't understand.   She finished the prayer and left the house.

Alicia felt Danny's presence in the house but wondered why he hadn't showed himself.   He would in good time.   Alicia walked over to a mirror that was on a door by the spacious living room. She was wearing a green and white gown which had one of the Adinkra symbols for *Sankofa*.   One symbol was the bird reaching towards its back which meant to go back and fetch it.   It meant it wasn't taboo to go back to retrieve knowledge in order to move forward.   The symbol on the gown was different.   It was the heart symbol of *Sankofa*.

Alicia was smiling to herself when her body started to vibrate.   She turned around and saw *HIM*.

Danny was standing a few feet in front of her in the entrance to the living room.   He was wearing an all-white linen shirt and pants.   The shirt was unbuttoned all the way revealing a perfect torso and six pack abs.   Danny's chocolate skin contrasted perfectly with his outfit.   Danny was in his bare feet.   She looked at Danny's head and saw that he had shaved his Caesar off.   The bald head made Danny's eyes stand out even more than they usually did. Alicia had to sit down.   She could barely breath.   She uttered one word upon sitting.

"Damn!"

Chapter 25

Danny smiled at Alicia's reaction to seeing him. He had planned everything down to the last detail. He purposely stayed away in order to build up her anticipation. He even brought in Akosua to help. Despite the slight unpleasantness of having to deal with Akosua, Danny felt everything went well. Alicia looked beautiful. She was ready for her first imprinting. Danny's masters had drilled into his head the importance of this moment. It was of the many things in which he had extensive training. "You haven't seen me in so long and all you have to say is damn?"

Alicia composed herself and smiled while allowing her eyes to take in all of Danny. "What did you expect me to say? It wasn't like I saw you last night. I mean look at you."

Alicia took in everything about Danny. The smooth chocolate face, and shaved head which made his almond shaped brown eyes stand out even more than they usually did. She felt butterflies in her stomach as she took in his muscular body. Everything seemed perfect from his broad shoulders, well-developed chest, and strong arms. Yes perfect indeed. This man was about to make love to her. Everything seemed unreal. Damn.

Danny walked over and held his hand out to Alicia. She took his hand as he pulled her to her feet. With a firmness she had never experienced before he pulled her to him and gave her a light kiss on her lips, and then another light kiss. He teased her with his juicy lips until she couldn't take it anymore and embraced him even tighter as their tongues explored each other mouths with an intensity Alicia had never felt before.

Danny pulled away very slowly and then gave her a light peck as if a signature to the long sentence of a kiss. He looked at Alicia with a gentle but powerful stare that penetrated her down to the depths of her soul.

Nothing was said.

Everything was understood.

Danny took Alicia's hand and led her upstairs to a bedroom. The bedroom door had the most famous Adinkra symbol painted on it. It was *Gye Nyame,* except for God. It represented the supremacy of God.

Alicia smiled as Danny pushed the door open and led her

through it.

The room was illuminated by several lit candles. There was a fruity aroma in the air that was making her feel some kind of way. There was soft jazz playing in the background. Any nervousness she had faded away.

Alicia looked around the room and saw a large bed with green and yellow sheets that had been pulled back. They were the colors of Het Heru, the Kemetic goddess of love.

Danny allowed Alicia to take in everything about the room. He felt her energy become more relaxed. She was ready for the next step.

Danny turned Alicia towards him. "Are you ready?"

Alicia looked into Danny's eyes, surrendering to his power and the moment. "Yes."

Danny lifted Alicia's gown over her head and allowed it to fall from his hand onto the floor. He stood back and admired her from her beautiful soft and feminine face, to her slender neck, her small but perky breasts with her engorged nipples. Danny took in Alicia's flat stomach leading down to the trimmed hair over her vagina. He had to maintain his composure as he looked at her shapely hips and legs. Damn she was a work of art.

Danny picked up Alicia effortlessly and laid her on the bed. Without taking off his clothes he got on the bed beside her, propping himself up on his left arm. He held his right hand six inches over her breasts and started moving his hand up and down very slightly without touching her.

Alicia immediately started feeling mild sensations in her body. "W...what are you doing?" She was not only feeling heat coming from Danny's hand but also his eyes as he slowly looked her up and down from her beautiful face to the top of her toes.

Danny looked at Alicia very lovingly. "I'm looking for you inside of me. When I find you then I can start making love to you."

Alicia giggled. "An action hero and a philosopher."

"I can make a ham sandwich too if you ate swine."

They both laughed as Danny began to move his hand up and down Alicia's torso. The energy began to fill Alicia's very being as her body began moving involuntarily. After a few minutes she felt a mild spasm in her breast area. Danny smiled as he noted her reactions. The spasms spread to her throat and stomach area and then she began having spasms in her cervix.

"Ohhhh!" The first orgasm took Alicia by surprise. It was the same energy she felt from Danny in the club but way more intense. The second, third, and fourth orgasms came quickly and with rising intensity. She tried to keep count of the orgasms but gave up after the thirtieth or was it the fiftieth? Alicia felt spasms through her body as she twisted and flung her arms and legs while Danny remained a rock, steady and firm while Alicia was in the throes of ecstasy.

How long did this go on?

Twenty minutes?

Thirty minutes?

Several hours?

Alicia lost track of time.

Even when Danny stopped moving his hand back and forth and just looked at her, the orgasms kept coming until Alicia was able to lay still. Fully at peace.

Danny got off the bed and stood in front of Alicia, treating her to a full view as he began to disrobe. He first took off his linen shirt revealing his muscular torso. Then he slowly took down his linen pants revealing a fully aroused manhood and the strongest, most powerful legs Alicia had ever seen on a man. Danny could have easily been a model.

Danny climbed back into bed using his powerful arms to support himself so his full weight wouldn't be on Alicia. Without any guidance the head of his manhood found the perfect fit in Alicia's vagina causing her to gasp softly. Danny penetrated very slightly moving slowly and rhythmically in and out of Alicia's sweet spot. He did this eight times bringing Alicia immense pleasure.

On the ninth thrust he slowly and gently thrust his entire manhood into Alicia. "Ahhhh" was all she could say as she arched her back and dug her fingers into Danny's back. As Danny pulled back slowly he felt two intense cervical contractions that sent waves of pleasure throughout his body.

Oh yeah Alicia was about to have many more orgasms.

Danny settled back into a rhythm of eight shallow thrusts and one long one as their bodies began to move as one. Once again Alicia lost track of time as the shallow thrusts slowly gave way to long rhythmic thrusts. As wave upon wave of pleasure rippled throughout her body, Alicia raised her legs and allowed Danny to pin her ankles by her head. The orgasms began to come fast and furious, one/eighth of a second at a time as her cervix began to contract to a steady beat. Then it happened.

Steam decided to join the party.

Danny could tell by the look in her eyes that the Steam was

fully present and didn't want the nice and easy lovemaking. Oh no, that was for Alicia. As a woman climbs the orgasm plateau she doesn't want that nice, polite, rose petal, and wine sex.

She wants the primal male.

Danny saw the look in Steam's eyes. She couldn't tell him with words. She was fully into her right brain at that point. The left brain was shut down. Everything was instinctual. She looked at Danny and communicated without words, "Take. This. Pussy!"

Normally Danny was the artist, the smooth cat, the pretty boy. Now it was Danny's turn to bring out another side to his persona.

Danny went into thug mode.

The look on Danny's face became intense as he was no longer merely thrusting with love and gentleness but was pounding like a warrior. Muscles started to ache as he had been propped up on his arms for a long time. It didn't matter. The true man ignores pain in both war and love. He fights through everything. He doesn't disappoint as he takes the woman through the highest levels of the tree of life.

The orgasmic energy overwhelmed Alicia as she let out a final gasp and blacked out as her body began to shake involuntarily. Alicia's vaginal grip squeezed Danny's manhood causing him to have several prostate contractions. It was only by Danny's sheer will and training in seed retention that he didn't ejaculate.

Danny pulled out of Alicia and laid on his back. He brought Alicia to him as they embraced as energetic ecstasy filled the room.

Chapter 26

Alicia propped herself up on her left arm as she looked at Danny's sleeping form. The night was incredible beyond belief. She was glad Danny was her first. She still felt his powerful energy inside of her. Alicia used her finger to gently trace around Danny's face. He was so physically beautiful and yet there was so much she didn't know about him.

Who is Danny Code?

Alicia slowly got out of bed and noticed that her overnight bag was in the room. So much was going on she didn't think about

it until then. She got out her tooth brush and went to the
bathroom to use the toilet and brush her teeth. Thankfully the
bathroom was connected to the bedroom so she didn't have far to
go. As she was walking she smelled breakfast being cooked.
Apparently they weren't alone in the house. Alicia used the facilities
and brushed her teeth. Then she put on the gown she had on the
night before, took one last look at Danny as he slept and quietly
slipped out of the room.

The smell of breakfast led her right to the kitchen where she
saw Mama Akosua cooking tofu that resembled scrambled eggs
with onions and red peppers mixed in. Also on the stove was
seitan style "bacon" along with freshly baked rolls. Also there was
a freshly made fruit concoction made from mangos, oranges, and
pineapples. The sight of the vegan food brought a smile to Alicia's
face.

"Like what you are seeing?" Akosua said. Even though her
back was to Alicia, Akosua felt her smile.

Alicia walked over to the stove to look at the food being
cooked. "Oh yes. Did Danny tell you I'm vegan?"

Akosua smiled as she looked at Alicia. "He certainly did.
Even if he didn't I would have cooked you something vegan
anyway." Akosua winked at Alicia.

For a brief second Alicia thought Akosua reminded her of
somebody. She just couldn't think of who that would be. Maybe
it would come to her later. "Thank you. I really appreciate this."

"Anything for Danny. He wanted your first time to be
special."

Alicia blushed. "He told you it was my first time."

"Not in so many words. Plus I can see things. It's amazing that you or rather that other spirit with you made it this many years without having a man touch you. Especially being a dancer."

Alicia blushed even more. She was surprised she was so comfortable with Akosua. "Did Danny tell you I was a dancer? Did he tell you about Steam?"

Akosua turned off the burner on the stove and used a spatula to put the tofu "eggs" onto a platter. "No. Truth be told Danny told me very little about you other than you being vegan. As far as the other things...I'm very good at reading people and whatever else is around them."

"I see." Alicia looked at the food. As fascinating as Akosua was she was ready to eat. She wasn't sure if she should wait for Danny or just dig in.

"Danny will be down soon. The smell of food is good to wake him up," Akosua said happily.

It seemed to Alicia that Akosua knew Danny on a deeper level. She was about dig deeper when Danny walked into the kitchen wearing a plain blue t-shirt with matching lounge pants and leather slippers. Danny was even fly while coming for breakfast.

"We were just talking about you," Akosua said with a mischievous grin.

Danny glared at Akosua.

"Relax...Danny. I didn't share any of your deep dark secrets."

Danny studied Akosua for a second and then looked at Alicia showing a rare smile. "How is everything?"

"Great, very great." Alicia wanted to run and jump into Danny's arms but restrained herself.

"Don't hold back on my account. I'll leave you two kids alone. Danny, text me if you need anything. I'll be up the path."

"Thank you Mama Akosua." Danny smiled a tense smile.

Alicia wondered what was up between these two. Akosua seemed very familiar with Danny and yet Danny seemed slightly uncomfortable around Akosua.

After Akosua left, Alicia grabbed Danny and kissed him fiercely.

Danny slowly pulled away from the kiss and looked Alicia deeply in her eyes causing a mild orgasm.

"Uh can we at least eat this wonderful looking breakfast first," Alicia said.

"I guess that would be a good idea," Danny said.

They laughed as they got out plates and utensils.

****

After breakfast and another session of making love that ended in the Jacuzzi that was next to the bedroom, Danny and Alicia decided to take a walk around the large house. Alicia wore a causal long sleeve shirt and loose jeans. Danny had on some khakis and a light weight sweatshirt. Alicia was very curious about the house.

"So is this a bed and breakfast?" Alicia asked as she looked at the large house. It looked big enough to house several people comfortably.

"No just a house that belongs to a group of people I've...worked with before."

"The Sankofa Collective?"

Danny looked surprised "You've heard of them?"

"That brotha I told you about, Baba Kofi, wanted my mother to join."

"Interesting."

"How did you meet them?"

"I've taken some classes with them on different subjects. I learned the energy projection techniques from one of their healers."

"Wow. Small world." Alicia and Danny began holding hands as they walked towards a small pond that near the house. "Not many people have heard of the Collective."

Danny shrugged. "They're very low key. They don't like drawing attention to themselves."

They got to the lake and found a spot on the grass to sit down. It was very serene. Alicia turned to look at Danny.

"Danny tell me who you are. Rather who you were before you became Danny Code."

Danny smiled. "My birth name was Matthew Evans." Danny told her about his mother, Gloria and how she had been a dancer. He talked about his mother's death and how he grew up in the foster care system. He told her about the sexual abuse he suffered at the hands of Mrs. Berry. Danny talked about the books he had read and how he decided to call himself Danny Code.

Alicia hugged Danny. She was grateful he shared so much of his real self with her. Maybe one day he would be comfortable talking about his real connection to Mama Akosua.

Chapter 27

Jeffery's face maintained a calm look while processing the words that came out of Bianca's mouth as they sat in the café where they met for lunch. Outwardly Jeffery looked unmoved as he sat wearing a dark gray suit with a matching tie and crisp white shirt. He looked like he could have been at a board meeting. Inwardly he was seething, using all of his will power not to explode and make a scene.

"Did you hear me?" Bianca said as she sat across from him in a blue business pants suit. "I said I don't want to continue this relationship."

Jeffery breathed in and out slowly. "I heard you very clearly. Why do you want to break up?" He wondered if Bianca would make any reference to Elias.

"Are you kidding?" Bianca surprised herself and Jeffery with the steel in her voice. "Jeffery what we have isn't a relationship. I'm not sure what it is. You say we're in a relationship but all we do is go on dates and to events where you need to be seen with someone. I mean we barely kiss. We certainly haven't had sex…"

"So this is about sex?"

"Please let me finish," Bianca said with even more resolve in her voice. "The lack of sex isn't the most important thing. It's the lack of intimacy. How many times have I been to your house? For all I know you live in a basement in a rundown neighborhood. How many times have you actually been inside of my condo? Answer me please Jeffery."

Jeffery's mask began to crack as there was a slight uncertainty in his eyes. "No I haven't had you over to my house. No I haven't been inside of your home."

"That's my point Jeffery. It's not about sex, or the events. In a little over a year we have never spent any real time with each other. I mean just doing things that ordinary couples do. Taking walks. Going shopping together. Sitting around watching a dumb TV show. How often have we really talked? I mean really talked about anything other than the event we were going to or the play we attended. When have we really connected?" Bianca thought back to when she met Jeffery at that charity event for the center for abused and neglected children. She was there representing her bank. She was impressed that Jeffery had made a big donation to the center. She had seen other millionaires make donations but she saw genuine caring in Jeffery's eyes. She was drawn to him for that reason. It didn't hurt that he was what her mother would have wanted for her daughter.

"So we can spend more time together." Jeffery had a brief look of desperation in his eyes. He then regained his calm mask. "You have already made up your mind?"

Bianca nodded her head. "Yes"

Jeffery let out a breath of air. "There's another man involved isn't there?" He thought about telling her that he saw her with Elias.

"This isn't about another man. It's about us. What we have does not work. I want more in a relationship. I want to be someone's woman. Not an escort. Not a beard."

"A beard?" Jeffery raised one eyebrow. He noted that she didn't really answer the question.

"Sometimes a gay man will go out with women in order to appear straight."

"A...are you saying I'm gay?" Jeffery really struggled to maintain his composure this time. He was many things but he felt zero attraction to men.

"I'm not sure what you are Jeffery. I'm not even sure you know. I just know I wasn't feeling the love."

"That's it then?"

"Yes Jeffery it is. If we were a normal couple I would give you back things that were at my condo and make arrangements to pick up stuff from your house or wherever you live." Bianca knew her words would sting but she was feeling bolder than ever. "Since we weren't a normal couple this is goodbye. Have a nice life. Maybe you can find what you looking for."

Jeffery watched as Bianca turned and walked out the door. No fanfare. She just left. Jeffery stared into space for a seeming eternity and then pulled out his smart phone to make a phone call.

****

"You starting to come by a lot lately. I might have to start cooking more," Jeffery's mother, Sharon, said as she opened her front door to let her son in. She had on a red silk bathrobe and her hair was slightly messed up. Jeffery frowned as he walked past her. He recognized the look from his childhood. She had just recently had sex.

Jeffery walked into the living room and immediately sat down on the couch. "Is he still here?"

Sharon sat down on the couch close to Jeffery. "I sent my entertainment home. He ran off like a good little boy. Hopefully he will develop more stamina. Maybe he can join your gym." Sharon giggled at the thought.

"Mother please." Jeffery leaned forward and buried his head in his hands and dry heaved a few times.

Surprising both Jeffery and herself, Sharon leaned closer and put her right arm around Jeffery's shoulders while using her left hand to stroke his hair. "What is it baby? Let it go."

Jeffery held his head and had tears forming in his eyes. "Bianca broke up with me." He regretted saying anything to his mother about the breakup. He expected her to say something mean.

"My poor baby," Sharon said with compassion in her voice. "It must hurt. I know in your own way you cared about her."

Jeffery wiped the budding tears from his eyes. "Yes I did."

Sharon hugged her son tightly. It wasn't the sensual hug that he was used to getting from his mother. It was a genuine motherly hug. "What did she tell you?"

Jeffery shrugged. "She said some things about not spending quality time together and not having sex. Some stuff. It's kind of a blur now. She didn't answer me directly when I asked her about another man."

Sharon released the embrace and moved back a little from Jeffery. A different look came over her. Gone was the nurturing woman who held him for a few too brief moments. Sharon was no longer in pure mommy mode. The manipulative bitch side of her came out coupled with the nurturing instinct. She was in mama bear mode now and someone had hurt her cub. "It seems to me this man has caused you some heartache. You two would still be together but for him. Think about it son."

Jeffery nodded his head. "Yeah. Everything was okay until he came along. Whatever we had Bianca didn't have any complaints."

"I told you last time you were here about your LaCroix blood. You have to deal with this Jeffery. It's about honor. It's about your manhood. A man has to do whatever it takes to regain his honor. I know your father taught you that as well."

"Yes he did." Jeffery smiled at the memories of the talks he used to have with his father. He wished his father was still alive.

Sharon turned Jeffery's face towards her. "Baby. Whatever it takes." She pulled his face to her and kissed him on his forehead. She then hugged him tightly. He was putty in her hands.

****

Jeffery immediately went to the safe built into the wall of his bedroom's walk-in closet. It was a high-tech safe that required a handprint in order to be opened. He placed his hand firmly on the screen to be scanned. The safe door opened and there was a few stacks of one hundred dollars bills, and some important documents. Jeffery didn't come for those things. He came for a gift his father had gave him when he was young, a nine-millimeter gun.

Chapter 28

Bianca wrapped the cord around the vacuum and then put it into the hall closet. She shook her head as she looked at her mother's freshly vacuumed carpet. Her mother's apartment would be a mess if she didn't come over to clean. Usually it bothered her but today she cleaned with a new lease on life. Even her mother who had been sitting in the living room in her night clothes and bathrobe noticed.

"Why are you so happy?" Wanda liked seeing her daughter smile. Though there was always some tension between them

Wanda wanted her daughter to be happy and to live the life she didn't have.

Bianca closed the closet doors. She was dressed very casually in a T-shirt and sweats. This was dressed down for her. Even when she cleaned around her mother's apartment she would wear some jeans and a nice blouse. Bianca smiled and sat down across from her mother on the love seat. "Yeah…about that." She tried to keep a serious face but she kept smiling.

Wanda thought she knew the answer. "Did Jeffery finally propose!?!" She could barely contain her excitement. Her daughter marrying a light-skinned millionaire Black man. It was like hitting the lottery. Maybe they would move her out of this apartment. It was nice but with Jeffery's money she could do better. Way better.

Bianca sighed. "No mother he did not propose. I'll just come out with it. I broke up with Jeffery."

"You what?" Wanda couldn't believe her ears.

"I said I broke up with Jeffery."

"Why would you do something like that? Did he hit you?"

Bianca sighed again. "No mother Jeffery did not hit me."

"What's the problem then? Did he cheat on you? Bianca dear, men are going to be whoremongers. That's how they're built. As long as he provides for you and is discreet about it you can live with it."

"No. Mother. He. Did. Not. Cheat." Bianca didn't want to get into the sex life or lack thereof with Jeffery. This was getting tiring with her mother. Bianca breathed in and out slowly. "Mother, the thing between Jeffery and I simply was not working."

"But Bianca you two looked great together," Wanda whined. "He was the perfect man. The perfect Black man. You know there's a shortage of men for educated, intelligent Black women such as yourself to date and marry. You're going to simply walk away from him?"

"Yes I am."

"Are you crazy!?!" Wanda was beside herself. She sacrificed too much to simply let Bianca blow this opportunity.

Bianca understood in that instance what people meant when they said they had a moment of clarity. Her whole life really was never about her. She knew that intellectually and rationally but never felt it in her spirit until then. "No mother for the first time in my life I feel what's really going on. This isn't about me and Jeffery. This has always been about your dreams and aspirations. Have you ever really cared about what I was about?"

"Bianca I just wanted the best for you. I wanted you to have what I didn't have. What is wrong with you?" Wanda's voice raised slightly. "Why would you give up a man like Jeffery Tyler? I mean think about him."

"Really mother? What's so special about him?" Bianca sat back in the love seat. She knew what her mother was going to say.

Wanda sat forward a bit. "Do I really have to tell you? Maybe I do since you are willing to make the biggest mistake of your life."

Bianca smiled.

"First of all," Wanda said, "Jeffery is a multimillion dollar African-American man. How many of them are there who are not playing with balls or singing and dancing? He's not a clown out there entertaining some white folks. He made his money through hard work. Very few men, Black or white, can say that. Second he's a handsome man. Most Black men out here are nappy headed, dark, and ugly. He has a nice beautiful complexion and with pretty hair and eyes. You two would make pretty children."

"You really don't know that mother."

"They wouldn't be fat, black, and ugly...I'm sorry Bianca." Wanda regretted her words.

Bianca to her own surprise was very calm. "Don't be mother. It's what you feel. It's what you been carrying inside of you all of your life. Tell me though what makes me fat, black, and ugly?"

Wanda let out a breath. "Bianca you're a big girl. You've always been big. You're not one of the slim pretty girls. Your weight and skin tone are not right."

"So do I have an ugly face?" Bianca was still very calm.

"No you're very cute for a dark girl."

Bianca chuckled a bit. "Whatever you do mother don't ever say that again to me or anyone else. So you're saying that if I was light complexioned and slimmer I would be beautiful?"

"Yes Bianca," Wanda said as tears welled up in her eyes.

"Mother, I truly understand where you are coming from. You came up in a different time. Understand this though. My complexion or my weight or rather my curves don't make me ugly. There is no one way to be beautiful. A rose and an orchid are two very different flowers and yet they are both beautiful. A slim light-skinned woman and a curvy dark skinned woman can both be beautiful. It just depends on who's looking at them. It also depends on how they feel about themselves. I'm comfortable with my size. It's how God made me. Are saying he made a mistake?"

Wanda gave Bianca a puzzled look. "I never thought about it like that."

"If I do say so myself I'm quite shapely. I have an hourglass figure. Even if I didn't and had a little more around my stomach would that make me any less beautiful? It's all about my spirit." Bianca thought back to a conversation she had with Elias about the beauty of a person's spirit. She understood it at the time intellectually but now she felt it in her spirit.

Wanda looked at her daughter intently. "Who have you been hanging around lately?"

"What makes you ask that?

"That sounded like it came from somewhere other than you."

"Or you mean it didn't come from you. Mother all my life I've told you what you wanted to hear. I've been your mirror. Maybe it's time you started hearing what's really on my mind."

"So you're going to start listening to other people?"

"You don't get it do you?" Bianca shook her head. "I'm going to start being free. I've lived your life long enough. It's time I started living for myself." Bianca stood up and walked to the closet to get her bag and jacket.

"What about me?" Wanda didn't know what to do. She invested so much in Bianca.

Bianca got her light weight sweat jacket out of the closet and put it on. She walked to the door, opened it and then turned to her mother. "It's time for you to start living your own life. My life begins now."

Chapter 29

Elias wondered why his mother was getting dressed so early on a Saturday morning. He was getting dressed himself to go into the store. She's been acting strange for the last week or so. One thing he noticed was that she was toning down her clothes. She usually wore short dresses and tight jeans. He heard one guy in his store call it "thot gear." "That hoe over there." Young people call things the way they see them Elias thought as he checked his clothes in the mirror. He had on a brown t-shirt with the phrase "Educated Brotha" in big white letters going across the front and some regular jeans. His sister said he needed to get some skinny jeans so he wouldn't look like a bamma. Elias told her he just got to look like a bamma then. Besides with the way styles come and go his look will be the rage in five years. Maybe then he would wear skinny jeans. Elias really hated following the crowd. That's why he couldn't work for anyone.

Elias took one last look in the mirror and left his room. He heard faint singing coming from downstairs. Was that his mother?

He walked down the steps and saw his mother in a plain blue blouse and some loose fitting jeans sitting on the couch. Loose!?! Was this his mother? She was also wearing some sensible heels? Hold up!

He listened carefully to what Debbie was singing. It was a church hymn he heard on the radio, "This Light of Mine." Elias could hardly believe his ears. Was he in a parallel universe? "Debbie?"

Debbie looked up and smiled, "Hey baby boy."

Elias looked at his mother and noticed that she had very little make-up on and her hair was done very conservatively coming down to her shoulder. She must have had a haircut recently. "Okay what have you done with my Debbie?" Elias chuckled to himself. To him the name Debbie meant mother.

"Don't worry I'm still your Debbie." She kept smiling.

Elias sat down next to his mother. "What happened?"

"You happened Elias. Our last major conversation made me think about a lot of things. You were right. I need to grow up. I'm the mother of a beautiful son and daughter. I have to start carrying my weight. I can't have my son take care of me the rest of my life."

Elias just looked at his mother. "This is so drastic though. Not that I'm complaining but how did this come about?"

"You didn't know but last week I went to church with your aunt Edna during the week. I didn't join or anything but it was refreshing to be around a different group of people."

"Whose church Auntie Edna go to?"

"She attends "Victory in the Gospel Sanctuary.""

"Reverend Leroy Gaston's church? Are you kidding me? He's nothing but a pimp in the pulpit. Don't you have to pay admission to get in?"

"Now baby, calling him a pimp in the pulpit isn't nice."

"You're right. I shouldn't insult pimps like that."

"Now Elias you're not going to give me trouble about going someplace that worships the white man's God as you call it?"

"Despite my personal feelings I'll support you whether you are worshiping Jesus, Mohammed, Buddha, Galactus, or the Great Pumpkin."

Debbie laughed. "The Great Pumpkin. I betcha one of those dusty hotep brothas that come to your store believes the Great Pumpkin is real." She laughed even harder.

Elias laughed with her. "Aw sista you don't know do you? See the Great Pumpkin was created by a conspiracy between whitey, the Jew, the coon Negro, the alien Greys, and Majin Buu."

"Wayment." Debbie had a mock look of seriousness on her face. "Majin Buu? I thought that was a cartoon character from *Dragonball Z?*"

"Nah sistar. That's what the Illuminati wants you to think." It was Elias' turn to have a mock look of seriousness on his face. "See Goku was real. He was a Black man whose real name was Gus. When he became a Super Saiyan instead of his hair becoming long and golden his afro would puff out black and strong."

Debbie couldn't keep a straight face and started giggling.

Elias continued. "Now you want to know why Majin Buu was up in there. See the cartoon was really a code for the conscious Black man to decipher. Majin Buu was defeated by Super Saiyan 3 Goku, ahem I mean Gus. The number 3 is the key. Three times three is nine. Nine times three is twenty seven. Two plus seven is nine. Nine divided by three is three. Three is the number of the original trinity. Ausar, Auset, and Gus."

"Bullshit," Debbie said to Elias and they both burst out laughing. They laughed for several minutes and then gave each other a hug. Elias needed this. He thought back to how they used to be at times before his father was killed. Yes Debbie acted like a child. Yes Elias wished she would have behaved more like an adult. There were times though when they would make each other laugh.

Elias finally stopped laughing long enough to regain his composure. "So Debbie you still didn't tell me why you are dressed up this morning or for you dressed down."

"I'm sorry I didn't tell you. I'm going to a church picnic with a man I met at church."

Elias thought that though he could see his mother was trying to change she would still be able to attract men. "So what's he's like?"

Right on cue the doorbell rang. Debbie got up and walked

to the door, opened it and let a man in and gave him a somewhat chaste hug.

Elias thought that maybe Majin Buu really was in the mix messing with him.

Debbie invited the man over to meet Elias. Elias appraised the man very quickly. He was definitely older but in great shape. He had a short salt and pepper haircut that flowed nice into a very well groomed beard. Elias could tell that the man was an athlete when he was younger. One thing that struck Elias was that the man was very different from the other men Debbie brought home. One he had all of his teeth. Two he really was in great shape and judging from his clothes employed. Elias was liking him already.

"Elias this is Frank." Debbie brought the two together. "Frank this is my son Elias."

Elias extended his hand which Frank took. "Nice to meet you man."

"Likewise," Frank responded.

Elias noted that Frank had a firm grip. A man's grip. "So what do you do for yourself?"

Debbie gave Elias a look. "Now *Dad*." He always did this with the men she brought home.

"It's okay Debbie," Frank said. Frank knew the game from when it was just him and his own mother. Elias wasn't going to let just any ol' man push up on his mom. Elias was only doing what he was supposed to do as a man. Frank liked Elias already. "I own an auto repair shop. You need that truck fixed I'll give you great service and great prices."

"Yeah," Elias said. "Next time I need some work done I'll

bring it by." Elias had a good feeling about Frank. "Hey you two have a good time. We have to sit down and talk later. Black men who own businesses have to network."

Frank nodded his head. "That we do. You are welcome to come to church sometime."

Elias chuckled, "That might be another conversation."

Frank looked at Debbie with a puzzled look.

Debbie winked at Elias and then turned to Frank. "My baby worships The Great Pumpkin and something called Buu."

"Huh," was all Frank could say.

Debbie and Elias both burst out laughing while Frank wondered what the joke was.

The healing between mother and son had begun.

Chapter 30

"That's great that you are mending fences with your mother," Bianca said to Elias as they walked around the mall. She was wearing a lightweight sweater and some jeans.

Elias smiled. "It's just a beginning. Me and Debbie got a lot to work out." He had on his "Educated Brotha" T-shirt and jeans.

"You call your mother by her first name?" Bianca was

surprised. She couldn't imagine calling her mother, "Wanda."

Elias shrugged. "She never taught me to call her mother. Part of the problem was that she didn't really accept being a mom."

"Now she does?"

"I think she is willing to try. That's all anybody can do."

"Mothers are a trip aren't they? I mean they can either nurture us to success or screw us up for life," Bianca said while shaking her head.

"You know, even the bad ones can inspire us to succeed." Elias let out a breath. "I had to get my hustles together because I knew Debbie wasn't adult enough to do things for us. It made me grow up before my time."

Bianca took Elias' hand. It felt good to him. "I think you did okay."

"I think you did okay too." Elias looked at Bianca and gave her a quick kiss. A few months ago they wouldn't have been able to walk around in public holding hands and kissing. The thought brought a smile to his face.

"What's so funny Elias?"

"Just how far we've come baby. Both of us."

"Yes we have." Bianca gave Elias a quick kiss. "You're beginning to resolve your issues with your mother and I'm finally stepping out from my mother's control to live my own life. It feels good."

"Yes it does."

"We have no place but…" Bianca sighed as they walked past a store featuring clothes for larger women. Bianca didn't like the selection in the store.

Elias saw where she was looking. "Don't worry about this place. There are other stores for real women."

"You mean Big Girls. I accept myself and my size." Bianca thought for a second and then smiled. "Elias I need your help."

"Anything baby. I got you. What do you need?"

Bianca took a deep breath and then let it out. "You remember when we talked about me opening a store for bigger women?"

"We mentioned it and were going to talk about it but I kinda forgot as I was riding your beautiful booty."

"You so nasty," Bianca smiled. "Well I've been thinking about it. I want to do it. Of course I have no experience running a store but I figure you can help me."

Elias looked at Bianca for a few seconds with an expressionless look on his face. He then broke out into a big grin. "Oh man Bianca. We can do that thing up. Get some real funky clothes up in that joint. I got some contacts from my vending days. We can get some pieces up in there that you can't find in any store. Trust me we can do this."

"So you'll help me?" Bianca was always a little nervous that Elias wouldn't help. She had never done something like this before.

"Baby it would be my honor." Elias gave Bianca a big hug and held her tightly for a few moments. Words couldn't express how proud he was of her at that moment. "Let's get out of here."

"What about your store?"

"Nzinga can run the store. She act like she don't need me there anyway."

Bianca laughed, "Well she do act like she own the place. I think she likes you too since she always gives me the side eye when I come in there."

"Nah, she just don't like bourgie sistas."

"What!?!"

"Don't worry about her. Let's go back to that park we hooked up at a while back."

"You want to go back to the park?"

"In many ways it put us on this path."

Bianca smiled. "You have a point there. Let's go."

****

A few hours earlier.

"Danny I like the energy of your place," Alicia said. She had just put her clothes on after she showered following lovemaking with Danny. She was dressed casually in a T-shirt and jeans.

"Thank you." Danny had on a long sleeve athletic shirt and some loose jeans. He was sitting wide legged on his couch.

Alicia sat down and snuggled up next to Danny. It had been two weeks since she lost her virginity and as fantastic as that first night was, the sex had got better. "I really do like the energy of the place."

"It's nothing special," Danny said non-chalantly.

"Danny you're just too cool. This place is…different." Alicia looked around the living room in the apartment. There was the couch they were sitting on and other than a computer work station there were two bookcases filled top to bottom with books as well as several books stacked neatly by the computer work station. The books themselves interested Alicia.

Given Danny's profession as a graphic artist there were several art books and manuals on graphic design. There were also several books on spirituality particularly eastern and African traditional forms. There were even some books on early Christianity and Islam. What really caught Alicia's eye was the books on warrior cultures from around the world. It seemed Danny had more of those types of books than anything else. It made sense with the paintings done by Danny that were around the apartment.

There were paintings of Japanese Samurai, Native American braves, and Maori warriors. Most of the paintings were of African warriors. She immediately recognized the paintings of Zulu warriors and of the Kanem Bornu Knights. There were many paintings of the same type of warriors but Alicia didn't recognize them. "Danny who are those warriors in those paintings. I recognize the others but not those." Alicia pointed to three paintings that were on the wall above his computer work station.

"Those," Danny said, "are Asanteman warriors of the Ashanti Empire from West Africa. The Ashanti Empire existed in the area that is now primarily Ghana. Asanteman went toe to toe with the British during the Anglo-Ashante wars in the 19th Century. We hear about warriors like the Samurai and maybe the Zulu but a continent as vast as Africa had many great warrior traditions."

"You're fascinating Danny Code." Alicia gave Danny a kiss

and for a brief second his eyes reminded her of someone else's eyes. She just couldn't think about who at that moment. She thought it would come to her eventually. "You're an artist, a healer, and you have the spirit of a warrior. I would almost think you were genetically engineered."

Danny smiled. "You read too much science fiction." He sat up. "Hey let's go to our favorite bookstore. I haven't been there because this beautiful woman has been occupying my time."

"Really who would that be?" Alicia gently stroked Danny's face.

"Just this goofy but pretty young woman who likes to read all the time and shake her ass to pay her bills."

"Very funny Danny. Let's get out of here before Steam pops up and kicks your ass for being smart."

****

The mall's parking lot while Elias and Bianca were walking around.

Jeffery sat quietly in the old Buick that had been purchased using cash. The car was registered in the name of someone that did not exist. One thing he learned from his father was that it was always good to have shady associates in case something needed to be done underground. "People who know people" as his father would say. The car wouldn't be traced back to him. Neither would the nine millimeter that was tucked safely in the glove department. Jeffery parked the car so that he would have a clear view of Elias' truck. So many things were running through his mind. If anything went wrong he could lose everything. It would have been way easier to hire a professional to handle this business. Jeffery needed to do this with his own hands. If all went right he would get away Scott free. Most importantly he would have his honor back. Maybe then his mother would love him.

Chapter 31

Elias and Bianca

"This is crazy," Bianca said as she climbed into the passenger seat of Elias's Ford Explorer.

Elias closed the truck door once Bianca was seated and secure. He moved quickly to the driver's side, jumped in, and started the truck. "Yeah it's crazy but then up to this point our relationship has been everything but normal. Why start now?"

Bianca smiled. "We're going to have to start doing things

more like regular folks. We don't have to sneak around anymore."

"Really," Elias frowned a bit. "Do you really think Jeffery is going to let you go like that? Between what you told me, what I've read about him, and when he was in my store a while ago he's not the type of man who will give up on what was his that easily. Hell most men are like that really. We need to keep our guard up at least for a little while."

"I know Jeffery has a rough side but I don't think he'll be a problem."

"Um hmm. You didn't see his eyes when he was here. I'll be on guard." Elias put the truck into drive and pulled out of his parking space. "Forget about that bamma right now though. The next few hours is about us. Baby will you back that thing up?"

"You so nasty." Bianca smiled broadly as she anticipated the next few hours.

As Elias drove to the entrance of the mall's parking lot he didn't notice that an old beat-up Buick had started following them.

Jeffery

He was surprised when he saw Bianca get in the truck with Elias. This complicates matters a bit. Dealing with one was trouble enough now he had both to deal with. Maybe for him to regain his honor he needed to kill both of them. Elias for disrespecting him and Bianca for betraying him. Was this the way to go though? His mother would say yes in order to regain his honor. She would say follow through to the end. Jeffery had to finish this. He needed to be a man.

Danny and Alicia

"Danny can I ask you something?" Alicia was very relaxed in the passenger seat of Danny's Mustang.

"Sure sweetie," Danny was very focused on the road but he had a gut feeling that something significant was about to happen. He hadn't had those feelings since he was a young boy.

"What's up with you and Mama Akosua?"

"What do you mean?" Danny's calm state immediately became defensive. Alicia could literally feel the energy shift.

"I mean what's up? I can see there's some tension between you two."

Danny kept his eyes on the road. That feeling he had made him sensitive to everything going on outside of the car. "Alicia I'm not going to insult your intelligence. I care too much for you to do that. That being said there are still some things about me that I'm not ready to share. I do hope I can...shit!"

Alicia sat up in her seat. "What wrong?"

"That white Ford Explorer that just passed going the other way was being driven by Elias with some sista in the passenger seat. A couple of cars behind them was Jeffery Tyler." Danny made a quick U-turn with a speed that astonished Alicia. Nothing about him suggested he had reflexes that fast.

"Jeffery Tyler? The millionaire? You know him." Alicia had a surprised look on her face.

"Yeah I know him. I designed his website and hung out with him a few times. Even brought him to the strip club on a day you were off. He was very uncomfortable though so we never went back." Danny looked frustrated as they got caught at a red light. He had a bad feeling about Jeffery following Elias.

"Why would he be following Elias?" Alicia was trying to make sense of everything.

"It all make sense now. You knew Elias was messing with someone else's woman. That was probably that woman in the Explorer. A few weeks ago Jeffery had come to the store and looked like he and Elias was about to come to blows. I diffused the situation but never got a chance to follow up. Jeffery must be ready to finish the job. No telling how far he is willing to go."

The energy in the car shifted. Danny knew what that meant. "Hello Steam."

"Danny. Time to lace up the Tims. Elias is my family. I can't let him be hurt."

"Come on light, change." Danny was starting to get anxious.

Elias and Bianca

Elias parked his truck in the parking lot of the small park in Camp Springs, Maryland, where he and Bianca once had some very intense sex right out in the open. Even though it was getting dark it was still light enough for something exiting to happen. After this they could make love like normal people. He would even get his own place. His abandonment issues were starting to heal after him and mother reached their understanding.

Elias walked around to the passenger side to help Bianca out of the truck. Once she was out they embraced and gave each other a long passionate kiss and then looked into each other's eyes. They began walking to the picnic tables that were a small field length away from the parking lot. As they were walking they heard a car pull into the parking lot.

"Damn we may not be by ourselves this time," Elias said with disappointment.

"We got all night. Being with you is good enough. Let's keep walking." Bianca was happy just to be alone with Elias.

Jeffery

Maybe God wanted him to regain his honor as well. Why else would Elias and Bianca go to a secluded park? This way he could do what was necessary and still get away. He could also look both of them in the eye when he pulled the trigger.

Elias and Bianca

"It looks like we're going to have some company," Elias said as he looked at the figure getting out the car. Something didn't feel right. Elias' street sense started to kick in. He hadn't carried a gun since he was hustling as a teenager but he wished he had one now. The figure was moving fast towards them. Could this be a stick up? "Bianca have a seat on the bench. I don't like this."

Elias watched as Bianca sat down. He assessed the situation. He wasn't armed and since the state did a good job of keeping the park clean there wasn't any loose bottles around or any branches that could be used as weapons. If this dude was armed Elias would have to talk his way out of getting shot. Thankfully he only carried a bank card and a little cash. Nothing that couldn't be replaced.

As the figure got closer Elias decided not to wait. "Yo what's up playa?"

"Nothing playa," Jeffery said as he stepped into view holding a nine-millimeter gun.

Elias, Bianca, and Jeffery

Elias and Jeffery stared at each other for several long seconds. It was Bianca who broke the silence. "Jeffery what the hell are you doing!?!"

Jeffery looked past Elias to Bianca. "Regaining my honor. You left me for him? This nigga got a little store and you want him over me. Do you know who I am?"

Bianca shook her head as she responded. "Apparently I don't."

"I will not be disrespected by either one of you." Jeffery pointed the gun from Elias to Bianca and back to Elias.

"So you gonna get your honor back by killing us." Elias glared at Jeffery. This wasn't the first time he had gun pointed to him.   For true to game hustlers it was a part of the life.

"Whatever it takes." Jeffery breathed in and out.   It was now or never.

"Jeffery what the fuck you think you doing!?!" a voice yelled.

Jeffery saw Elias and Bianca look past him. He turned to his side slightly to see who was coming. It was Danny Code and a young woman.   Danny looked different from his usual stoic self. Both he and the young woman look like they were ready for war.

Elias, Bianca, Jeffery, Danny, and Steam/Alicia

Danny calmly walked past Jeffery and stood in front of Elias.   At the same time Steam walked to Bianca and gently pulled her to the side.

Jeffery was trying to maintain his cool despite everything falling apart. "What are you doing here Danny? I'm not going to let you stop this like you did last time."

Danny glared at Jeffery with an ice-cold stare. Jeffery had seen the look before in a contract killer. Who the hell was Danny Code?

"Get out the way Danny. I don't have a beef with you. You didn't cheat with my woman. You didn't take my honor."

Danny spoke in a measured tone.   "So this is about honor? You really think you're going to get your honor by shooting this man? You not even holding that gun right. Despite how close you are you would still miss. You're not a shooter. Give me the god damn gun." Danny held his hand out.

"I could just shoot you too," Jeffery tried to sound confident but inwardly he wasn't so sure.

Danny was eerily calm. "You could try but I didn't take your honor. This man did." Danny surprised everybody by indicating Elias. "Killing me won't give you anything. You'll just be a murderer. If you want your honor back you must deal with Elias. Again give me the muthafucking gun. Don't make me take it from you."

Jeffery looked at Danny intently. Something about how Danny made that last statement suggested that Danny could indeed take the gun from him. Jeffery walked closer to Danny and handed him the gun. Danny immediately took out the clip and popped out the one bullet that had been in the chamber. He then walked over to the picnic table and laid the pieces on it. All eyes were on him as he walked between Jeffery and Elias.

Danny looked at Jeffery and then he looked at Elias. "See we have a problem here. Jeffery has a point. Elias you were sleeping with his woman. You disrespected his boundary. Wars have started over a man's boundaries being violated. Elias, Jeffery has every reason to be angry with you. A man's boundary is everything."

Elias glared at Danny, but remained silent because he knew he was right.

Danny turned to Jeffery. "Your instinct to reclaim your honor is correct. The way you were going to do it was incorrect. If you had a gun Elias needed to have gun. For you to be armed and not Elias is the way of a coward. The Jeffery Tyler that built a million dollar business is far from a coward."

"You're right. I'm not a coward." Jeffery glared at Elias.

"There's the thing about your honor.   This ends one way tonight."   Danny stepped back a few yards and looked at both men. "Knuckle up!"

Chapter 32

Jeffery backed away from Elias and after a hard look unzipped the hoodie he had been wearing to reveal a plain black T-shirt. The veins on his arms were huge as he revealed a well-muscled torso. Jeffery rotated his head back and forth making a cracking noise with his neck. Oh yeah he was ready to go.

Elias regarded Jeffery's pre-fight ritual and was not impressed. He rolled his shoulders and danced on his toes a bit never taking his eyes off of Jeffery.

Bianca couldn't believe these two men were about to fight.

For a brief second she admired Jeffery's muscular body. She had never seen him like this before. Maybe if she had things may have been different. She whispered to Steam standing beside her. "This is crazy. These two grown men are about to fight over me."

Steam gave Bianca a side eye. "Check your ego. This is deeper than you. This is a male thing as old as time itself. These two may have fought over a parking space."

Bianca gave Steam a look. She wasn't sure if she was going to like her. "This is still crazy."

Steam's persona switched to Alicia in order to ease the growing tension between the two women. Steam didn't want to have to give Bianca an unnecessary ass whipping. "Let it play out sis. My name is Alicia by the way. Elias is like my brother. Other than my blood brother he's the only family I have."

Bianca thought her mind was playing tricks with her. The eyes on the woman before switched from hard and aggressive to soft and vulnerable. "Bianca. Pleased to meet you." She turned to the two men who were about to fight.

Danny Code was taking in everything around him. He felt Steam shift to Alicia which diffused another potential fight. Good he could focus on the two men in front of him. "Remember no matter what y'all feel about each other y'all still warriors and you have to abide by a code."

They both nodded to Danny and then began circling one another. Elias threw his hands up first leading with his left as he cocked his right. He moved slowly towards Jeffery jabbing into the air to gage the reaction.

Jeffery raised his guards up mirroring Elias as he led with

his left fist and held his right fist close to his chin. He jabbed with his left a couple of times to gage Elias' reaction. Jeffery noted Elias' fighting stance and how he was holding his hands. Elias was a definite street fighter but not someone who has had the same training he had.

Danny picked up on Elias' fighting stance as well. Good enough for the streets but not against someone who has had training like Jeffery has obviously had.

Suddenly Elias went at Jeffery throwing a flurry of jabs and hooks. He managed to land a blow to Jeffery's jaw but not enough to knock him out. He did land a few body shots including one to Jeffery's ribs.

Jeffery gritted his teeth in pain. Elias surprised him with his ferocity. Jeffery smiled. No need to hold back.

Jeffery came straight at Elias jabbing first with his left and then landing three straight jabs with his right fist to Elias' jaw knocking him to the ground. Elias was dizzy on the ground and instinctively covered up expecting Jeffery to come right at him. When he looked up Jeffery simply danced on his toes. He didn't move to finish him.

Jeffery smiled at Elias. "Get your ass up."

Elias rose to his feet quickly and lunged at Jeffery. The two men exchanged a flurry of punches to each other's face and bodies. Jeffery dodged a wild swing from Elias and caught him square in his nose knocking him to the ground. Jeffery was satisfied with the blood coming from his opponent's nose until he felt some blood in his mouth. One of his teeth felt loose.

Bianca couldn't believe what she was seeing.

Alicia was doing everything she could to keep Steam from jumping in.

Danny kept calm as he watched these two men both of whom he respected beat the crap out of each other.

Elias rose slowly to his feet. This time it was Jeffery who rushed in furiously with several combos that put Elias back on the ground. Jeffery backed up as he watched Elias struggle to get back up. This time he wasn't smiling as he was in a lot of pain himself.

Bianca couldn't take anymore and yelled at Danny. "Please stop this fight."

Danny and turned and glared at Bianca. "They have to stop this themselves. Stay out of this!"

Bianca was shocked at how Danny looked at her. First Alicia and then this man. These were Elias' friends? What kind of people did he hang around? She felt a hand on her arm. It was Alicia.

"Don't take it personally," Alicia said. "Men are fond of saying, 'let a man be a man.' This is one of those times."

Elias rose to his feet with blood streaming down his face and onto his clothes. It would have been so easy to stay on the ground. There was no shame in taking a beat down. He had his share growing up as well as giving a few. Something though was driving him to keep standing back up.

Jeffery was breathing hard as he looked at Elias. The anger that had originally driven him to want to kill this man was no longer there. It was replaced by something else, admiration. If their positions were reversed he would have done the same thing. In some ways it was like he was fighting himself.

Elias stood in front of Jeffery. He strained to raise his fists to defend himself. Jeffery slowly raised his fists and with a burst of strength stepped to Elias and put his power into a hard punch to the jaw. Elias fell to the ground and lay there for a seeming eternity. Elias then started to slowly get on his feet and then he fell to the ground again.

Jeffery walked over and stood over Elias as he lay on the ground. He then stooped and grabbed Elias and lifted him up to his feet. Then in a surprise move gave Elias a tight hug.

Bianca couldn't believe what she was seeing. Neither could Alicia. Danny understood the meaning right away.

Jeffery broke the hug and stepped back from Elias. "I can't beat you without killing you. I yield." Jeffery put his right fist out and then covered it with his left hand and then bowed to Elias.

Elias put out his right fist and then covered it with his left and returned the bow to Jeffery.

"Gentlemen," Danny placed his left hand over his right fist and then bowed to both Jeffery and Elias.

Bianca didn't know what to make of what she was seeing.

Alicia just smiled.

Danny looked at Jeffery. "Congratulations. You have your honor back. His life was in your hands. Yet you imposed your will over your lower nature. That's what it means to be a man."

"Thank you," Jeffery said to Danny.

Elias stood in front of Jeffery. "You never hit me while I was down. You could have killed me. What really stopped you?"

Jeffery paused before responding. "Your heart."

"My heart?" Elias asked.

229

"No matter what you wouldn't stay down," Jeffery said. "Men with heart like that are rare. We need to work out our differences in a different way. Me especially I need to deal with why I'm here to begin with. For all I think I'm about the only reason we are both here at this time is because I allowed my mother to manipulate me."

At that moment everyone stopped and looked at each other.

Chapter 33

They all stood around looking at Jeffery as they tried to process what he just said. Bianca spoke first.

"Did you just say your mother manipulated you into this foolishness?"

Jeffery looked at Bianca and nodded solemnly.

"All of this because of your mother?" Bianca couldn't believe her ears. "The few times I met her she did seem…sneaky. I felt like she was constantly sizing me up."

Jeffery took a deep breath. "That's my mother. I told her

about you and Elias." Jeffery took another deep breath. "She made me feel like I had to do something to regain my honor. I don't know what she wanted to gain." Jeffery sat down on the grass with his knees propped up and holding his head in his hands.

Bianca sat kneeled down on her knees beside Jeffery. "But why would you let her do that? You never seemed like the type of man who would follow someone, even his own mother."

Jeffery looked at Bianca. "That's just it. She's the only person who could push my buttons. We weren't particularly close as I was growing up especially as my parents divorced. Then there was this one ...incident."

Danny immediately recognized the look in Jeffery's eyes. It brought up the sexual relationship with his own foster mother, Mrs. Berry. Even in his thoughts Danny didn't want to think of her by her first name.

Bianca put a hand on Jeffery's shoulder and asked softly, "What happened?"

"She tried to seduce me! Her own son." Tears welled in Jeffery's eyes. Normally he would never show such weakness but he didn't care at this point. He looked at Bianca. "I didn't touch you because I'm... that...thing...did something to me. I'm just not sexually attracted to anybody. It was never you. I'm sorry if I made you doubt yourself. You're a wonderful woman. I sincerely wish you nothing but happiness."

Bianca reached over and hugged Jeffery. Jeffery found the hug to be very warm and caring.

Elias had a "huh" look on his face. "So you mean to tell me that you were going to shoot me and then you fuck my ass up because of mommy issues?" Elias paced around for a few seconds as all eyes were on him. Elias let out a breath and then looked at Jeffery. "You know I should be pissed at your yellow ass but believe it or not I'm not. Yeah you had your mommy issues but then so did I."

Alicia walked over to her friend and squeezed his hand. Elias smiled in response and then looked at each person briefly before looking at Jeffery.

"I don't have a mother doing some soap opera shit and trying to get me to kill a nigga, I mean N-word," Elias said. "Nah she just wasn't there as a mother. She was more like my sister or sometimes like my kid. When I'm not acting like I'm a street n…brotha, I'm reading all these deep books. It turns out I have serious abandonment issues. One way they come out is that I'm afraid to live by myself. I have my mother and sister living with me for no other reason than I'm afraid to be alone. I also drink more than I should to fill the void."

Elias sat on the grass across from Jeffery and Bianca. "I'm facing my issues though. I will be getting my own place soon, or moving my mother and sister out, whichever is easiest. Then I'm going to talk with this substance abuse counselor I know. I mean I haven't abused alcohol but I'm right at that line. I don't want to cross it."

Jeffery nodded his head. "You won't cross it. You're too much a warrior." He looked up at Danny who nodded an affirmation.

Bianca sat back a bit. "You two aren't the only ones with mommy issues. My mother tried to control every aspect of my life.

I had to be her perfect little girl and I was just that. I realized recently though that I had to live for me. Jeffery I wasn't with you for the right reasons. You were my mother's vision of the perfect man for her perfect little girl. It wasn't fair to you. Will you forgive me?"

"Yes," Jeffery responded. "If you will forgive me."

Bianca smiled and reached out to hug Jeffery again. She knew she would never be sexually attracted to Jeffery but she felt like they could truly be friends.

Alicia decided to join the conversation. "You know I didn't have the same mommy issues as y'all had. Mine were daddy issues. My biological father was never around and my mother's boyfriend molested me. I, or rather my other self, Steam, worked as a stripper in order have control over men. I didn't want to be scared again and not in control." Alicia looked at Jeffery. "I was even a virgin until recently." Alicia instinctively glanced over at Danny who seemed like he was blushing through his chocolate skin.

Elias stood up and hugged Alicia. "Girl I thought you had that glow." Elias with his left arm around Alicia's shoulder held out his right fist to Danny. "My nigga."

Danny slowly gave Elias a fist pound while trying to hide a sheepish grin. "What makes you think I'm the one?"

"Even I can see the connection between you two," Jeffery said.

Everybody laughed, even Danny.

Bianca looked up at Danny. "So are you like the rest of us?"

Danny looked at everyone. "I was raised in the foster care

system though people thought my foster mother was my real mother because we had the same eyes. Only problem with my foster mother was that she saw me as more than a foster son."

Everybody immediately caught Danny's meaning and didn't want to press any further. There was a long moment of silence until Elias decided to speak.

"You know I don't believe in coincidences," Elias said. "Things happen for a reason. The five of us are here at this place and time for a reason. I can't speak for your individual spiritual beliefs but in mine I believe that we are all here to grow in spirit and to help each other grow. I mean we have a street kid who became a bookstore owner, a metaphysical stripper, a millionaire, a bourgie chick, and ...Danny who the hell are you anyway?"

Danny smiled, "That might be a long story."

"I'm sure you'll share it with us one day when we all meet for brunch. My point is that there is something bigger going on here. As we go forward we have to remember that."

Elias walked over to Jeffery and held out his hand to help Jeffery up. He then gave him a one armed hug. "Yo I know we started off as rivals but I think I can learn from you. I want to expand my business as well as help Alicia and Bianca get their businesses off the ground."

Jeffery looked at Bianca. "You have a business idea? Why didn't you tell me?"

Bianca stood up and shrugged her shoulders. "I'm just coming up with an idea. I want to open a store for curvy and thick women with some stylish clothes. I want to leave the banking field. That corporate life was something my mother wanted. It's not for me anymore."

"I will definitely help you," Jeffery smiled and then looked at Alicia. "I want to help you as well even though we are just meeting. As Elias says, 'we're all here together for a reason. What is your idea?"

"I want to open a juice bar where poetry can be read with maybe herbal tea and whatnot," Alicia said. "I have a lot of money saved but there are so many things I would need."

"We can work something out," Jeffery said. He felt a new lease on everything though there was still one problem he had to deal with.

"This group therapy session is cool and everything but it's getting dark out here. We need to take this conversation elsewhere," Danny said.

"Maybe a coffee spot," Alicia said.

Elias looked at the blood on his shirt and Jeffery's shirt. "Yeah...we might want to change clothes first."

Everybody laughed.

A beginning.

Epilogue

"My, my, you really are starting to visit a lot more," Sharon LaCroix said to her son Jeffery as he walked into her home and stood in her foyer. She was wearing a tight red t-shirt and curve hugging black jeans with some four inch heels. Jeffery was very casual with a baseball shirt and jeans.

Jeffery noted how his mother was dressed. Even when casual she had to be over the top. "I won't be here long. In fact you might not see me a lot in the next few months."

Sharon looked at her son with concern. "What are you

talking about?"

"I took care of that problem with Bianca and her new man."

"Really? So what did you do?" Sharon smiled. This should be good.

Jeffery paced around a bit before speaking. "I was going to do as you said. I had a gun to shoot the man who took my honor away."

This was turning Sharon on. "So did you shoot him?"

"No." Jeffery looked at his mother. She looked excited by the idea that he shot someone. No wonder he was so messed up.

"So what did you do?" Sharon was disappointed.

"We got into a fist fight."

Sharon perked up. "Really? Did you fuck him up?"

"I 'fucked' him up but I lost the fight."

"How the hell do you fuck him up but lose the fight? Explain that one to me."

"I yielded to him. No matter how much I pounded him he kept getting back up. I couldn't have truly beat him without killing him."

"And?"

Jeffery shook his head as he looked at his mother. "You talk about honor but you know nothing of it. You don't even care about it. I see your game. You don't care anything about me. You knew if I did anything I would ruin my life. Why would you do that to your own son?"

Sharon looked at Jeffery for several long moments and then started to clap very slowly. "For a man you aren't that dumb. You obviously inherited some smarts from me." It was Sharon's turn to pace around. She stopped in front of Jeffery and looked up at him. "You're a man. Why should I care anything about you or your species? I learned how men were early in life from my uncles who used to get me alone and do…things to me. I learned that men were weak because my father didn't protect me from his brothers. The only weapon I had was to manipulate you sick bastards. All of you."

Jeffery thought back to the conversation after the fight at the park. He began to feel pity for his mother. "I'm…sorry. I didn't know."

For a brief second Sharon had a soft and vulnerable look in her eyes but then they turned hard and cruel. "I learned early what men wanted and how to manipulate their weak minds. Your daddy though was different. He was strong minded. More than loving him I respected him. I couldn't break him. You have some of that in you. I couldn't break him but I wanted to break you."

"I'm your son," Jeffery sighed.

"You're a man," Sharon said cruelly.

Jeffery looked at his mother for a long time. He couldn't imagine what she went through to bring her to this point. "Two things. I came here to tell you that you lost. You will never be able to manipulate me again."

"Don't be so sure," Sharon smiled.

"Second, if you want therapy for your childhood abuse I will pay for it. I'm sorry you went through it and I will help where I can to heal you."

"So noble of you. The great Jeffery Tyler," Sharon said

sarcastically.

"I won't be seeing you for a while. I have my own healing to do. When you are ready for help contact me." Jeffery took one long look at his mother and walked out the door. With his back to her she couldn't see the tear streaming down his left cheek.

"Punk," Sharon muttered to herself as she slammed the door behind Jeffery. At least he wouldn't see the tears starting to form in her eyes.

Several Months Later

Alicia's Juice Joint was jumping on its opening day. Alicia with the help of her friends was able to make her dream come true of having a juice bar where poetry could be read. Bianca helped Alicia get a low interest bank loan to purchase a rundown commercial property on Georgia Ave. near Howard University. Elias helped her with the business structure and necessary permits. Jeffery really came through for her. It was Jeffery and one of his crews that renovated the property. It surprised her that this multi-millionaire businessman did most of the work himself. He said it was therapeutic for him to get back his roots. For a pretty boy he was good with a hammer. Danny, well it turns out Danny did have a weakness. He wasn't the type to put in dry wall or be handy with a paint brush. At least he kept making good love to her. He did create a great website for the juice bar.

It was crowded on the opening day. The patrons were a healthy mix of college students, bohemian types, poets from around the DMV, and surprisingly many of her former customers from the strip club.   Even a few of dancers made it through.

Alicia had on a green turtleneck sweater, some nice jeans and some boots with modest heels.   She was taking in everything when a hand tapped her on her arm.   It was her brother Solomon. He was wearing a dress shirt and some jeans.

"Hey Lish.   T-t-this is nice.   I'm very proud of you.   Proud of you."

Alicia hugged her baby brother.   "Ahhh thank you my love. This is all for us.   Soon we'll be able to get a place for both of us." A tear welled up in Alicia's left eye.

Solomon broke the hug.   "Lish who's that lady over there? S-s-she's very pretty."   Solomon pointed to a tall, chocolate, and curvy woman who was wearing a long purple sweater dress that clung to every inch of her voluptuous body.

Alicia looked over and saw Bianca and Elias.   What a couple.   Bianca was looking elegant and sexy.   Elias on the other hand was wearing a black sweatshirt that said, "Tantra Brotha" in big white letters and some jeans with basketball shoes.   Well at least he fit in with many of the bohemian patrons.   She motioned them over to her.

Bianca and Elias hugged Alicia at the same time.   Then Elias gave a one armed hug to Solomon.

Solomon however was paying more attention to Bianca. He wasn't shy about letting her know this.   "Hello there my queen. My name is Solomon."   He took Bianca's hand and kissed it softly making her blush.

Alicia was slightly embarrassed.   "Ummm Bianca this is my little brother Solomon."

"My, what a handsome young man," Bianca said.

"Thank you my queen. What I have pales in comparison to your radiance," Solomon said suavely.

Bianca smiled. "Oh my, a smooth young man."

"My Nubian goddess, allow me to get you something from our juice bar. It's on the house."

"Uhhhh," Alicia raised her hand slowly but then decided to let it go as she watched Solomon lead Bianca to the bar.

"Damn that little dude is slick," Elias said. "You notice he didn't stutter once. That's the power of the booty. Make a blind man see and an autistic kid a playa."

"No wonder she got you wide open." Alicia playfully elbowed Elias in his ribs.

"Well you know. Nothing like a good woman." Elias looked around at the club. "The grand opening is a success. Look at all these bammas in here. You did great. I'm so proud of you."

"I'm proud of you too baby. You haven't had a drink in months."

"You know it's been easy with the support of my friends. Ironically it's been Jeffery who really keeps me disciplined. It's funny that a man that was gonna kill me is keeping me sober."

Alicia looked over to the door. "Speaking of which here's Jeffery now."

Jeffery walked towards them wearing a blue sweater and gray slacks with some Italian loafers. Jeffery walked over, hugged and kissed Alicia and gave Elias a one armed hug. "Hello friends."

"Thank you for coming Jeffery," Alicia said.

"I wouldn't miss this for the world," Jeffery responded.

Elias looked around. "You did a great job fixing this place cause it looked like crap when Alicia first bought the property."

Jeffery nodded. "Thank you. Running a multi-million dollar company is one thing but I really loved breaking down walls in here and putting in toilets. I seriously think about selling my company and just being a contractor. I'm at peace when I'm fixing a house."

It was then that Bianca returned with a green smoothie in her hand. She immediately gave Jeffery a hug and kiss on his cheek. Ironically they were now closer as friends than when they were in a relationship.

"Where's your new boyfriend?" Alicia noticed that Solomon didn't return with her.

"I think he found another woman." Bianca used her eyes to indicate Solomon over by the bar talking with a shapely young woman with a nose ring and long locs.

Alicia, Bianca, and Elias burst out laughing. Jeffery just looked at them. "I think I missed the joke."

Elias looked at Jeffery. "It's just the power of the nani bruh."

"Yeah okay," Jeffery smiled. He turned to Bianca. "Your grand opening in a couple of weeks is going to look like this. I guarantee it."

"Thank you." Bianca looked at her friends who supported her as she left her banking job and helped her get her clothing store ready for its grand opening. She was going to truly be free. A thought occurred to her at that moment. "Where's Danny."

"He's on his way," Alicia said. "He said some business he

had to take care of first."

Who is Danny Code?

Danny parked his car in the bookstore parking lot. He had not been here in a very long time. He walked up to entrance of the store and looked up at the name. *Afrikan Renaissance.* He spent a lot of time here as a teenager. He walked in the store and memories of his time there began to flood into his consciousness. He immediately went to the café section of the store and sat down at a table. The place was unusually empty. He overheard one of the workers saying that many of the patrons were checking out the new place that opened, *Alicia's Juice Joint.* Another worker said that they weren't worried about losing customers as poets and boho types tended to show everybody some love. Danny was wearing a black turtleneck sweater, blue jeans and black boots. As he sat he closed his eyes and began to meditate as he waited for the person he came there to meet. He didn't have long to wait.

"Hello Kwaku," a familiar voice said.

"Danny. You know I don't answer to Kwaku anymore," Danny said as he looked up at Mama Akosua.

Akosua sat down. "Yet you did answer to your name and not Danny."

Danny glared at Akosua. "Technically my name is Matthew."

Akosua leaned back in her chair. She was wearing a beautiful mud clothe dress and some boots. Her locs were in a single braid going down her back. She sighed. "Okay…Danny."

Danny decided to be direct. "So why did you ask me to meet you here? Of all places."

"Was your time with the Sankofa Collective so bad?"

"No. I was trained to do many things. Maybe if I had a choice in the matter I would feel differently."

"We always have a choice...Danny."

"Did I? You took a homeless orphan and trained him to be an assassin."

Akosua sighed. "Is that all we did? Yes you killed many men. But were you a murderer? Or a soldier in a 3000 year old war that most people don't know anything about? Every man you killed was a soldier in that war. Agents of the Circle. It was them or you."

"Did it ever occur to you that maybe I didn't want to fight in any wars? Maybe I just wanted to live my life as I saw fit."

"Isn't that want you're doing now? We have left you alone. We were content with doing that until you reached out to us to help you entertain your girlfriend with the split personality. Why did you reach out to us...Danny?"

Danny let out a breath. "I don't know. I really don't."

Akosua looked at Danny. "I know it was tough. I know we...I... used questionable methods to train you. Everything was done to unlock the potential of you and your fellow participants in the project. We didn't just train you to be a killer. You know that. We also unlocked your creativity which you now use to make money. We unlocked your third eye so that you could see ahead and anticipate what was coming. And the main thing we unlocked your sexual potential which was the key to everything else."

245

"Yeah but the way you unlocked it…"

"Did you really think a young girl could unlock your potential? A young girl wouldn't know how to make love to you. Get your mind out of that so-called western thinking. We are at war. Desperate times call for desperate measures."

Danny looked at Akosua. "Why do you really have me here?"

"We need you back Kwaku. You were one of our best. The Circle is starting to develop a new breed of warriors."

"The Collective hasn't developed new warriors to combat the Circle?"

"There's been some …issues. We've had some defections. Some of our warriors have switched sides and joined the Circle."

"So now you have these brothas who are advanced martial artists with energy projection abilities now fighting for the other side? Nice. It's not my problem."

"Kwaku…Danny…whatever you want to be called. I know you feel some kind of way towards me but it was for the greater good. I want you to think about it. We need you. We won't pressure you. Just think about it."

Danny looked at Akosua for a few tense moments and then stood up. "I will think about it but I won't make any promises."

Akosua smiled. "That's all I can ask. Have a good evening K…Danny."

"You have one as well Mrs. Berry."

About the Author

Who is Rom Wills? I have had many words used to describe me. I've been called mysterious, brilliant, and goofy. I'm the type of person who can read a comic book in the morning and an obscure book on deep metaphysics in the evening. I can hang out on a street corner one moment and with powerful movers and shakers the next. I can talk about the read option offense in pro football and the inner workings of the national economy the next. I can say without conceit that I could star in some "Most Interesting Man in the World" commercials. I'm formally educated with advanced degrees and yet my best education has come from simply living life. There are very few things I haven't either personally experienced or know someone who has experienced certain things. My life would make a very compelling movie.

So who is Rom Wills? I'm a man who is on a mission to make a difference in the lives of the people I touch. Everything that I have experienced in life, good and bad, has been a life lesson. Through my writings, lectures, workshops, or talking trash in a barbershop I strive to share something that will positively impact the people around me.

Rom Wills is the author of the international bestseller Nice Guys and Players, and the follow-up, Sexual Chemistry.

Follow Rom on the World Wide Web:

www.romwills.com

Facebook.com/Willspublishing

Twitter: @RomWills1

www.ingramcontent.com/pod-product-compliance
Lightning Source LLC
Chambersburg PA
CBHW031107260626
47172CB00001B/259